"Obeah" and
Other Martinican Stories

Ruth Simms Hamilton
AFRICAN DIASPORA SERIES

The Ruth Simms Hamilton African Diaspora series at Michigan State University Press presents the past and contemporary experiences of African people throughout the world, written by emerging and established scholars in various fields in the social sciences and humanities in pursuit of a reconceptualization of the historical global movements of African peoples. This series pays tribute to the life and legacy of Dr. Ruth Simms Hamilton, a pioneer in African Diaspora Studies, and builds on her seminal work and conceptualization of the African diaspora.

The series editors are particularly interested in innovative book-length manuscripts grounded in scholarly research and inquiry that challenge both preexisting and established notions of the African diaspora by engaging new regions, conceptualizations, and articulations of diaspora that move the field forward. In underscoring new frontiers and frameworks in the study of African descendants' lived experiences, the series presents new approaches to the production of knowledge on African diasporas. In keeping with the tradition of the field, the series is an interdisciplinary undertaking devoted to scholarship on the histories, political movements, institutions, cultures, intellectual discourse, ways of knowing, and identities of African and African-descended peoples. Since the diaspora is based largely on movement, the transnational migrations of Africans throughout history and in contemporary times have complicated what it means to be black and or African depending on the political, economic, religious, geographical, and cultural context Africans find themselves. As a result, scholars are forced to confront the evolving realities and constructions of blackness and Africanness in a changing world. While much of the scholarship in the diaspora continues to focus on the Americas due to the enduring legacy of the Middle Passage and trans-Atlantic slave trade, in addition to these areas the editors encourage manuscript submissions that bring greater visibility to less studied but nonetheless critical areas of the Africana world. This includes internal diasporas within the African continent and African diasporas of the Indian Ocean, Pacific, and European regions.

The series highlights the global experiences and dynamic dimensions of peoples of African descent. It maps their historical and contemporary movements, speaks from their radical (unique) narratives, and explores their critical relationships with one another. By exploring Afrodescendents within their particular and broader sociocultural, historical, political, and economic contexts, it contemplates similarities, difference, continuity, and transformation.

COEDITORS:
Glenn Chambers, *Michigan State University*
Quito Swan, *Howard University*

EDITORIAL BOARD:
Afua Cooper, *Dalhousie University*
Gerald Horne, *University of Houston*
Franklin W. Knight, *Johns Hopkins University*
Besi Muhonja, *James Madison University*
Cheikh Thiam, *The Ohio State University*
Robert Trent Vinson, *The College of William and Mary*

"Obeah" and
Other Martinican Stories

Marie-Magdeleine Carbet

Translated and edited by E. Anthony Hurley

Michigan State University Press · *East Lansing*

♾ The paper used in this publication meets the minimum requirements of ANSI/ NISO Z39.48-1992 (R 1997) (Permanence of Paper).

All material is published with the permission of Marie-Magdeleine Carbet's estate.

Michigan State University Press
East Lansing, Michigan 48823-5245

Printed and bound in the United States of America.

26 25 24 23 22 21 20 19 18 17   1 2 3 4 5 6 7 8 9 10

LIBRARY OF CONGRESS CATALOGING-IN-PUBLICATION DATA IS AVAILABLE.
ISBN: 978-1-61186-237-9 (paperback)
ISBN: 978-1-60917-519-1 (PDF)
ISBN: 978-1-62895-289-6 (ePub)
ISBN: 978-1-62896-289-5 (Mobi)

Book design by Anastasia Wraight
Cover design by Erin Kirk New
Cover image: Marie-Magdeleine Carbet

Michigan State University Press is a member of the Green Press Initiative and is committed to developing and encouraging ecologically responsible publishing practices. For more information about the Green Press Initiative and the use of recycled paper in book publishing, please visit www.greenpressinitiative.org.

Visit Michigan State University Press at *www.msupress.org*

To Dorothy, my forever love (d. 19 July 2016),
and to Dr. Yolande Marie-Magdeleine,
Anna's beloved and loving niece

Contents

Acknowledgments

I AM SINCERELY INDEBTED TO LIANNE CHARBIT, WHO, AS MY GRADUATE student, contributed months of hard work, examining a mass of raw manuscripts, excluding those already published, and producing the first clean copies of Marie-Magdeleine's original stories, as well as the first raw drafts of the English translation. Lianne was also instrumental in reestablishing contact with Dr. Yolande Marie-Magdeleine in order to clarify some biographical details. Without Lianne, it is doubtful whether this volume would ever have been completed. I am also indebted to Dr. Nadège Dufort of East Tennessee State University, who provided invaluable help in my attempt to translate Martinican Creole words and expressions. Words are inadequate to express the gratitude and debt I owe to Professor Renée Larrier of Rutgers University for her consistent encouragement over many years and her gentle insistence that I complete this project. You are a power of example. Thank you so much, Renée. Finally, I have been privileged to be provided on a very personal and immediate basis with the assistance and support of my first reader, my loved and loving wife, Dorothy.

Introduction

IN THE COURSE OF RESEARCH INTO THE EXISTENCE OF FRENCH CARIBBEAN women poets who may have been writing and publishing during the first half of the twentieth century, I frequently encountered references to a M.-M. Carbet, who, I was to discover later, had produced numerous written works across a range of genres: collections of poetry, novels, short stories, and even cookbooks. In terms of sheer volume of output, this woman remains, at the beginning of the twenty-first century, Martinique's most prolific woman writer to date. M.-M. Carbet, I subsequently learned, was also a songwriter who had written a number of Creole songs and produced a number of records, including "Noël en Martinique" (Christmas in Martinique), performed by the "Petits Chanteurs à la Croix du Bois" (Little Singers at the Wooden Cross), and put to music for the Caribbean Creole singing star Moune de Rivel by the French pianist and composer Serge Lancen (1922–2005). Moune de Rivel, the stage name of Cécile Jean-Louis Baghio'o, born in Bordeaux in 1918 to Guadeloupean parents, is considered as the original grande dame of Caribbean Creole singing. This megastar has expressed the profoundest admiration and respect for Marie-Magdeleine Carbet, gives Carbet credit for opening her (Moune's) heart to authentic Creole music, and considers Carbet as the true ambassadress of the traditional musical culture of the French Caribbean (Antilles-Guyane).

Further investigation produced evidence that Carbet's extensive humanitarian and literary activities had earned her many international awards, including the Gold Medal from Belgium (Médaille d'or—Internationale—Délégation de Belgique), membership in the Academia de ciencias humanisticas y relaciones, the Palme d'or de Paris for the totality of her work, the European Silver Medal for cultural and artistic merit (Médaille d'argent: Mérite culturel et artistique européen), and France's Humanitarian Grand Prix for services rendered to arts and letters (Grand prix humanitaire de France pour services rendus aux Arts et Lettres).

As a writer, in the context of most literary histories of the French Caribbean, Carbet occupies a curious position in the literary universe of Martinique, dominated, in the opinions of most literary historians and critics, by such iconic male figures as Aimé Césaire, Édouard Glissant, Frantz Fanon, and Patrick Chamoiseau. Female writers and intellectuals, among them Mayotte Capécia, Suzanne Césaire, and Paulette Nardal, have attracted much less critical attention. Even Marie-Magdeleine Carbet, the author of several collections of poetry, including *Chansons des îles* (1937) and *Piment rouge* (1938) with Claude Carbet; *Point d'orgue* (1958), *Écoute, Soleil-Dieu* (1961), *Viens voir ma ville* (1963), *Suppliques et chansons* (1965), *Rose de ta grâce* (1970—winner of the 1971 Prix des Caraïbes), *Mini-poèmes sur trois méridiens* (1977); three novels, *Au peril de ta joie* (1972), *Et merveille de vivre* (1973), *D'une rive à l'autre* (1975); the short story collections *Ça et là dans la Caraïbe* (1937) and *Braves gens de la Martinique* (1957), published in collaboration with Claude Carbet; and *Contes de Tantana* (1980), as well as collections of songs and cookbooks, has remained relatively unknown.

M.-M. Carbet was for a long time a mystery for me. Who was this woman? And who was Claude Carbet? M.-M. Carbet's life and work evidently constituted an extraordinary story. How many Martinican women of her generation would have led such a remarkable life? Active participation in civil rights, animal rights, women's rights, anti-racism, and peace movements in Paris; working in the theater and in radio; writing prolifically in a variety of genres; teaching in Martinique; and apparently enjoying the personal experience of unconventional avant-garde freedom.

I had the privilege and joy of meeting this extraordinary woman on her bed in a rest home in Fort-de-France when she was ninety-two. Persistent inquiries had led me to make contact with her niece, Dr. Yolande Marie-Magdeleine—a medical doctor who had done part of her medical training in the United States—who arranged for me to meet her aunt and accompanied my wife and me on our visit to the rest home. I had heard stories before that Anna Marie-Magdeleine, for that was her given name, had been a strikingly beautiful woman, slim, tall, and elegant, often wearing a hat, with an overall extraordinary "allure."

Even in her nineties, suffering from an illness from which she was not going to recover, she was still an impressive figure despite the frailty of her body, with wide, clear, bright, twinkling eyes, thoroughly enjoying the visit from a strange man and his wife, even inclined to flirt. I still remember her last words to me: "Je suis toujours capable de m'enflammer" (I'm still capable of getting turned on). This playful and provocative interest in the opposite sex provides an interesting contrast with her preference of a living partner and also with the profound religious faith that she expresses so often in her writings.

On that occasion, Anna instructed her niece to allow me complete access to her library, provide me whatever permissions were needed for the reproduction of her published work, and entrust me with copies of all her published books (many of them out of print) and with previously unpublished handwritten and typewritten manuscripts. Included among these were extensive research notes for a volume she was preparing on French Caribbean writers, and a heavily revised manuscript of a history of French Caribbean literature. These documents revealed that Carbet was an ardent supporter of literary activities by some of her contemporaries and worked to have the works of one of her younger contemporaries, Paul Niger (pen name of Albert Béville, 1915–62), published posthumously. Niger was the author of a collection of poetry, *Initiation* (Paris: Séghers, 1954), and the novels *Les puissants* (Paris: Éditions du Scorpion, 1959) and *Les grenouilles du Mont Kimbo* (Paris: Maspéro/Présence Africaine, 1964).

Since the male writers who have lent their native land, Martinique, an international presence and renown have all been associated with sociocultural and even ideological theorizations, one question that arises for any individual who admits to the identity of Martinican is their positioning in relation to questions of identity politics. It needs to be emphasized that at the beginning of the twentieth century when Carbet was born, Martinique was still a colony of France. When the territory opted in 1946 for the status of Overseas Department, Carbet was in Martinique. It is no doubt significant that the change in the political status of Martinique is not reflected in her writings. This fact—this absence—suggests that such a change was apparently not particularly important to her and did not materially affect her self-concept or her relationship with either Martinique or France. One inference that may be drawn from this apparent lack of sensitivity to Martinique's political status vis-à-vis France is that probably Carbet was not materially different from many Martinicans who have been relatively content with, or resigned to, the formalization of integration, through departmentalization, into the French political and cultural ambit, and were never deeply troubled, before or after departmentalization, by any internal conflicts of cultural identity or of political affiliation with the metropole.

Biographical information on Carbet has been sparse and difficult to authenticate. The following details of her life have been substantiated in large measure by Anna's own documentation of her biography. Carbet was meticulous about keeping records of her literary and other public and professional activities and even constructed a chart of all these activities divided into separate columns: one column, "Literary Production," has subheadings for her publications with Editions Leméac, Montréal, with "Other Publishers," her "Collaborations with Claude Carbet," and her participation in a special issue of "Hommes et Destins"; a second column lists her participation in literary and artistic groups and social action associations; a third column lists "Plays and Cultural Activities"; a fourth column lists her "Conferences and Lectures"; a fifth column lists her "Professional Activity, Diplomas, and Medals"; and a sixth column lists other activities, including her collaboration with *Solidarity* magazine, her founding and editing of *Ceux d'Outre-Mer*, the creation of a literary prize associated with that magazine, and other published articles and collaborations. The care with which this chart was constructed and the many other listings of her activities in her own handwriting would suggest that Carbet anticipated or at least hoped that someday someone would be interested in details of her life and work, and she wanted to provide order and accuracy in the record of her life work. In addition to the information provided by Carbet's own documentation, other more personal details were supplied by her niece, Dr. Yolande Marie-Magdeleine, in writing and in telephone and face-to-face interviews, first with me and later with one of my graduate students, Lianne Charbit.

One of the first mysteries to be solved was the question of her name. I discovered fairly early in my inquiries that "Carbet" was not her official name. Her family name, I was told, was Marie-Magdeleine. Louise Eugénie Anna Marie-Magdeleine, called Anna, was born on August 25, 1902, in the inland village of Ducos, in Martinique. Her handwritten notes on her life indicate that she did not discover the sea until she was ten. Her parents, Eugène and Inès, called Aya, were of modest means. They were extremely hard-working folk, particularly her mother, a dressmaker who worked at night without electricity (which came to Martinique only around 1935 or 1936) in order to provide for their children the best possible advantages for success in life, particularly upbringing and education. Anna was the fifth of eight children: Cécile, Josèphe, Honorine, Edward, Anna, Mathilde, Laurence, and Gaston. She was particularly close to Edward, the brother who was born just before her in 1900, and this attachment is reflected in many of her writings. According to Anna, her childhood was very happy, even radiant (in her own words, "épanouie"), particularly because her mother, in her view, was an exceptional woman, kind-hearted, courageous, and intelligent.

Part of the mystery surrounding Carbet's surname is reflected in her father's experience. Her father, Eugène, was born in 1857. Slavery had been abolished only in 1848 and official records of that period were erratic. Eugène was the third of four sons of a married couple who bore the family name of Constantin. He was brought up by his parents with his brothers, and was apparently called Constantin at school. His father worked at the Mairie (City Hall) of Ducos, had fathered children from several women before his marriage, and recognized them all as Constantins. When, however, Eugène got married to Inès, the official record bears the name Eugène Marie-Magdeleine and not Constantin. After the marriage, however, Eugène continues to be called Constantin, and Inès is called Mrs. Constantin, although that was apparently not the "official" name that he had kept. Eugène died in 1929. The declaration of the Second World War, on September 3, 1939, by Britain, France, Australia, New Zealand, India, and South Africa proved to be a traumatic and fatal event for Inès, since she died that same month. When she received notice that her youngest son, Gaston, had been drafted into the armed forces, she called him and told him: "You're going to bury me before you leave." Two days later she had a stroke and eight days after that she died, surrounded by all her children, with the exception of her eldest son. He, Edward, the fourth child, had already met his end in Indochina, but neither she nor anyone else in the family knew anything about his death. The news reached them long after the invasion of the French colony of Indochina by the Japanese, July 24, 1941. He was an engineer who had built a bridge that the Japanese had to take in order to advance, and he was captured defending it. He died of cholera in a Japanese concentration camp.

Meanwhile, Anna began her formal schooling in the village, first attending primary school. From the age of eleven to seventeen, she continued her education as a scholarship student in Martinique's capital city of Fort-de-France. She received her Elementary Certificate at fifteen, and took her Secondary Diploma and Secondary School-leaving Certificate. By the age of twenty, she had received her teaching diploma and had started her teaching career as an adjunct teacher. She left the island for France for the first time around 1923, to continue her studies in Paris for four years for the C.A.P. (Certificat d'Aptitudes Professionnelles [Vocational Training Certificate]), working in the civil service while she was a student. She studied teaching domestic science, handicraft for secondary schools and colleges, and dressmaking. In addition to her pedagogical studies, she followed courses at the École de Beaux Arts (Fine Arts School) and at the École de Droit (Law School), as well as courses in journalism. In 1928, she returned to Martinique and taught at the Lycée de Jeunes Filles (Girls' Secondary School) in Fort-de-France until 1935 when she left once again for France, returning to Martinique on a ministerial mission in 1939, forced to stay as a kind of political exile.

Sometime after her return to Martinique in 1928, a friendship developed between her and a teacher of English, whose name has been variously reported as either Claude Tricot or Olympe Claude, a divorced woman who had a child, Peter. When in my early researches I had found references to publications by "Claude and Marie-Magdeleine Carbet," I had assumed that the authors would be a husband and wife, or even a brother and a sister. However, I have been reliably informed that Anna and Claude lived together openly in Martinique and France and published together three collections of short stories: *Féfé et Doudou, Martiniquaises* (1936), *Çà et là sur la Caraïbe* (1938), and *Braves gens de la Martinique* (1957), as well as two collections of poems, *Chansons des Îles* (1937) and *Piment rouge* (1938). From the collection *Chansons des Îles* they also produced a record of songs sung by S. Solidor. The association between these two women lasted for some twenty-five years. The awareness that two women in the Caribbean of the 1930s lived and published openly together, even daring to adopt the same family name, underscored their courage and exceptionality.

I have speculated elsewhere that the choice of the name "Carbet" used by this couple (see "D'un masque à l'autre: Marie-Magdeleine Carbet" in *Elles écrivent des Antilles*, ed. Suzanne Rinne et Joëlle Vitiello [Paris: L'Harmattan, 1997]) is significant for two important reasons. On one hand, "carbet" is the word used to designate the huts in which the "original" indigenous population of Martinique and of many of the Caribbean islands, known as Caribs, lived. Ruins of some of these dwellings have been found in the north of Martinique. On the other, "Carbet" is the name of a village in the north of Martinique. This term, therefore, is a strong signifier of Martinican identity. Consequently the choice of Carbet as a surname signals that the bearers of the name are profoundly Martinican.

By 1935, Anna was back in France, teaching in Paris with some breaks until her retirement in 1950, and engaging in a variety of professional and literary activities. She regularly attended the George Sand Club; participated in a variety of cultural groups, such as "Antillian Solidarity," "Gens de Lettres," and "SACEM" (an association of colonial writers); and founded the C.O.M. group (Ceux d'Outre-Mer [Overseas Club]). She also published articles and essays and served as a literary critic in the press. According to her own records, in 1937–38 Carbet participated in the production of what she notes as the first "exotic" broadcasts on Radio France from the Eiffel Tower. The term "exotic," I surmise, was used to designate the focus of the broadcasts on aspects of French Caribbean culture, considered from the perspective of metropolitan France as exotic. In 1938 a play, "Dans sa case," by C. M. Carbet (presumably a joint effort by Claude and Marie-Magdeleine), was staged at the Salle Jean Goujon in Paris. This production was arguably (and Carbet considered it as such) the first example of an authentic "Black Theater," created and produced by blacks, to be mounted in the French capital.

As a result of such activities, by the end of the 1930s Carbet had gained considerable recognition as a folklorist at the highest levels of government in France, as evidenced by the fact she was sent to Martinique by Georges Mandel in 1939 on a ministerial assignment to conduct research into folklore. It may be recalled that after the surrender of France to Germany in June 22, 1940, a new government was established under Philippe Pétain and the French capital was moved to Vichy. Georges Mandel had been Interior minister before Pétain came to power and was a vocal opponent of the Nazis. He was arrested and imprisoned by the collaborationist Pétain government in 1940. Anna's appointment by Mandel made her suspect under the Pétain government and she was prevented from leaving Martinique by the 1939–45 war. In fact, on the declaration of war, the mission that she had started came to an end. She resumed her position at the Girls' Secondary School, but was soon dismissed by the local representative of the Pétain/Vichy government, Admiral Robert.

After 1940, she participated in a number of social and political action groups, including AMITAG (Amicale des travailleurs antillais et guyannais—an association of workers from the French Caribbean and French Guyane), and CASODOM (Comité d'Action Sociale des Originaires des DOM [Social Action Committee of Natives of Overseas Departments]), founded in 1956.

In 1941, she opened a private school in Lamartine Street in Fort-de-France, focused on teaching English, remedial, and dressmaking courses, and even providing free lessons. The school closed in 1945. In 1945, Anna and Claude opened a bookstore, Cité du Livre, on Schoelcher Street in Fort-de-France. In 1957, the association between Claude and Magdeleine ended and the bookstore was sold. No explanation has been given for the ending of a relationship of more than twenty years. All that I have been told is that it was extremely painful for Anna.

In 1957, Marie-Magdeleine returned alone to Paris, where she began an intensive literary activity, publishing on her own. Between 1957 and 1970 she produced six volumes of poetry, records, and newspaper articles. She was on the editorial board and the national council of MRAP (Mouvement contre le racisme et pour l'amitié des peuples [Movement against Racism and for Friendship among People]). She also participated in international cultural groups, gave courses on literacy to new immigrants to France, and traveled extensively in the French provinces as well as internationally, including Mali, to lecture and attend conferences. She made numerous radio broadcasts on French Radio and wrote articles in support of her antiracist principles and in support of Antillean cultural specificity.

From 1970 to 1984, her literary activity switched to Canada, and she produced a series of writings published by Leméac in Montréal, where she also gave talks on radio and joined the Association of Catholic Writers. In 1988, feeling the burden of her increasing age, she returned to Fort-de-France with her sister Mathilde. Anna never married, never had children. She died January 10, 1996.

Part of the mystery that surrounds Carbet, apart from her name, is the lack of any acknowledged connection to the movement of cultural consciousness that was taking place in Paris in the 1930s—the Negritude movement—which has dominated the interest of scholars of Francophone Caribbean literature ever since. How do we explain the fact that, among such an extensive literary production on Carbet's part, there is no explicit reference in her work to Negritude or to the luminaries of the Negritude movement, such as Aimé Césaire or Léon-Gontran Damas, although it is clear that she was active in social and literary circles in Paris at that time? Even more puzzling is the question of Carbet's lack of participation in the periodical *La Revue du Monde Noir*, published by Paulette Nardal in 1932, particularly since Paulette was her sister-in-law, the wife of one of her brothers, most likely Gaston. The bilingual magazine had expressed as its mission to:

Donner à l'élite intellectuelle de la Race noire et aux amis des Noirs un organe où publier leurs œuvres artistiques, littéraires et scientifiques . . . [et] . . .

Créer entre les Noirs du monde entier, sans distinction de nationalité, un lien intellectuel et moral qui leur permette de se mieux connaître, de s'aimer fraternellement, de défendre plus efficacemennt leurs intérêts collectifs et d'illustrer leur Race. ("Préface," *Revue du Monde Noir*, 6 April 1932).

[To give the intellectual elite of the black Race and to friends of Blacks an organ for publishing their artistic, literary, and scientific works . . . [and] . . . to create, among Blacks the world over, without distinction of nationality, an intellectual and moral link that would permit them to better know one another, to love one another fraternally, to defend their collective interests more effectively, and to bring renown to their Race].

Carbet's active participation in MRAP suggests a sensitivity to issues of race and social justice. This sensitivity is reflected in dramatic and effective form in the poem "Greffe" (Transplant), which appeared in her 1970 collection, *Rose de ta grâce*. This poem is coincidentally dedicated to Paulette Nardal, a fact that underscores the relationship that existed between the two women, but which also heightens the dilemma of the lack of a direct contribution by Carbet to Paulette Nardal's publication. The poem, "Greffe," was stimulated by the 1968 internationally publicized account of the first heart transplant, when the South African surgeon Dr. Christiaan Barnard performed the open-heart surgery of successfully transplanting the heart of an accident victim into a male patient. The news report that stimulated Carbet's poem, and which she uses as a notation under the dedication, states: "En Afrique du Sud un coeur de nègre a été greffé sur un blanc par le professeur Barnard—Les journaux, janvier 1968" [In South Africa a black heart has been transplanted into a white man by Professor Barnard—Newspaper reports, January 1968]. Barnard's first successful heart transplant, on December 3, 1967, was that of a white female donor, Denise Darvall, into the body of Louis Washkansky, who survived only eighteen days. His second transplant, on January 2, 1968, was that of a young man (twenty-four years old), Clive Haupt, categorized as "coloured" under South Africa's apartheid laws, who had died of a cerebral hemorrhage, into a dentist, Dr.

Philip Blaiberg. The operation was a resounding success, trumpeted all over the world. Blaiberg left the hospital in March 1968, was soon able to drive his car, and blew out the fifty-nine candles of his birthday cake on May 24, 1969. Haupt's "black heart," as news reports specified, beat in Blaiberg for 563 days until Blaiberg died August 17, 1969. Carbet used the poem, based on this incident, as a vehicle to explore the ironies and wider symbolic significance of such an event occurring in South Africa, and to express personal solidarity with the condition in which black South Africans found themselves during that period of vicious apartheid:

> Et si mon cœur se souvenait?
> Marqué à jamais en ses fibres
> Du sceau des brûlures anciennes
> S'il se révélait étranger
> À tes angoisses, à ta haine?
>
> . . . .
>
> Si mon cœur de nègre emmuré
> Sanglé en poitrine de blanc
> Refusait d'endosser ta peau?
> Si de mon rire bafoué
> Il suffoquait . . . à t'étrangler?
>
> S'il te renvoyait à la gorge
> Crachats et mépris encaissés?
> Si brusquement en toi, montait
> Le fiel des humiliations
> Qui furent mon pain quotidien? (*Rose de ta grâce*, 19–20)
>
> [What if my heart remembered?
> Forever branded in its fibers
> With the stamp of ancient burns
> What if it showed itself alien
> To your anguish, and to your hate?
>
> . . . .
>
> What if my negro's heart immured
> Strapped into a white man's chest

Refused to endorse your skin?
What if on the jibes of my laughter
It choked . . . to the point of strangling you?

What if it threw back in your throat
The spit and scorn it had received?
What if in you suddenly rose up
The gall of the humiliations
That were my daily bread?

Even though Carbet's poetry is not dominated by explicit concern for resolving problems of identity, social injustice, or ideology, it would be a mistake to minimize her awareness of these problems and the challenges that these problems posed for her as a woman of color. The racial and sociocultural sensitivity that "Greffe" exhibits, for instance, was reflected in an earlier poem entitled "J'ai menti" (I lied), in which the poet asserts:

J'ai appris, dès les premiers pas
Que mieux vaut détourner les yeux
Des fronts exemptés de pigments,
Fussent-ils fronts de nouveaux-nés.

. . . .

Peuple nourri, gavé de leurre,
Dressé à se saouler d'espoir,
Asservi, tapes dans le dos.
À l'esclavage en travesti
Sous belles nippes tricolores.
Peuple courant après des ombres,
Insolentes caricatures,
D'égalité, de Liberté,
De l'amour dans la dignité.
Paix dans mon cœur?
Silence et lâcheté. Mensonge!
Il est tourment, tourment et plaie!
(*Viens voir ma ville*, 44–49)

[I learned, from the first steps I took,
That I'd better turn my eyes away
From faces that have no pigment

Even though they were the faces of new-born children.

. . . .

People fed and stuffed with deception
Trained to be drunk on hope,
Enslaved, blows on the back,
To slavery in fancy dress
In fine tricolored gear.
People running after shadows,
Insolent caricatures,
Of equality, of Liberty,
Of love in dignity.
Peace in my heart?
Silence and cowardice. A lie!
It is agony, agony and wound!]

The "silence and cowardice . . . agony and wound" expressed by Carbet certainly echoes the frustration and pain voiced by Aimé Césaire's poetic protagonist in *Cahier d'un retour au pays natal* in evoking the silence of his native land and his own complicity in rejecting the pitiful black man encountered on a tramway. Carbet, however, does not restrict herself to sociopolitical concerns. She is equally stimulated creatively by the world of the physical senses. The same woman who expresses this intense consciousness of social inequality and underlines the ironies of superficial conformity to principles that are constantly violated also expresses a similarly intense sexuality:

Tes lèvres font ouvrir des fleurs
De joie au vaisseau de mes reins ;
Sous mon front tremblent des lueurs,
Quand tu les poses sur mes seins.

Quand tu les poses sur mes seins,
Tes lèvres me vident les veines,
Et me font danser des essaims
D'abeilles tout au long des aines.

Des essaims d'abeilles sur l'aine,
Dans les entrailles du piment,
Dedans mon coeur et miel et peine,

Un cuisant, délicieux tourment.

Un cuisant, délicieux tourment
Que j'endure les dents serrées,
Tandis que s'enfle, sourdement,
Ton souffle ample et lent de marée.
("Tourment," *Point d'orgue*, 16)

[Your lips open flowers of joy
In the vessel of my loins;
Glimmers tremble under my brow,
When you lay them on my breasts.

When you lay them on my breasts,
Your lips cause my veins to drain,
And set swarms of bees
Dancing all along my groin.

Swarms of bees on my groin,
Pepper in my belly,
Inside my heart both honey and pain;
A burning, delightful torment.

A burning, delightful torment
That I endure with clenched teeth,
As all the while dully rises
Your breath, slow and ample like a tide.]

A particularly intriguing aspect of this poem is the fact that while the poetic persona who is voicing the poem is clearly female, the sexual partner in this poem is not identified textually by gender, so that the poem may be read as an expression of homosexual lovemaking by two women. The (deliberate?) masking of gender only serves to intensify the mystery in which Carbet is enshrouded as woman and as writer, and expands her imaginative and creative profile.

The brief and fragmentary biography that we have provided does not do justice to someone who was clearly a remarkable woman—a woman who lived a long and, in many respects, a veiled life. Who was Marie-Magdeleine Carbet? Even after her death we do not know. Her writings, both published and unpublished, do not provide enough answers for us to draw definitive conclusions. We are left with tantalizing questions. At age ninety-two, Carbet talked about "being capable of being turned on." If she was that frisky at that age, what must she have been like at twenty, thirty, forty, or fifty? Was she ever in love? What were her passions? Who were her lovers? Were they exclusively female? It would be justifiable to conclude that the woman who wrote a poem as explicitly sensuous as "Tourment" had experienced passionate sexual experiences. Also unanswered is the question of whether she had a position on Negritude. Clearly some of her writing attests to her positions in relation to racism and racial injustice, as "Transplant" exemplifies. She was born just a decade before Aimé Césaire, was in Paris during the same period that Césaire was there, and was one of the few Martinican women who published during that period. Why was she not included, as far as we know, in Césaire's circle, or why was Césaire not included in hers? How could such a woman become almost invisible?

Even the name under which Marie-Magdeleine Carbet publishes perpetuates the mystery. Why did she choose to use and retain two surnames, one her father's and the other linked to a woman's whose association with her ended (as far as we know) almost forty years before her death? There is, moreover, no consistent pattern in her writing that would allow us to draw conclusions about a single "true" Carbet persona, since this persona expresses itself variously in a movement from sensuous poetry, to passionate, almost militant discourse, to the almost radical religiosity of the short stories translated and presented in this book. One cannot even surmise that aging accounts for the transformation—that the sensuality of youth gave way to the religiosity of the aging. We cannot ignore the fact that it was the ninety-two-year-old woman who talked of being turned on by a man several decades her junior.

The mysteries that surround Carbet may never be resolved. Who, after all, can we ask? Not even her niece, Yolande, a wonderful source of information, can answer most of these questions.

So, in death as in life, Anna Marie-Magdeleine remains a mystery.

Our effort in this book is not to disclose the mystery of the woman but to acknowledge that she was a Martinican woman clearly before her time. She wrote, published, took stances and risks when few Martinican women, most notably the Nardal sisters, were bold enough to do the same. Yet, there are no conferences devoted to her writings, her name is rarely called, and there was little public acknowledgment of her passing.

This volume comprises seven short stories written by the most prolific female writer to emerge from the island of Martinique, one of France's Overseas Departments, including four that have never before been published. The four "new" stories were among a set of original, handwritten manuscripts and other documents entrusted to me by Mlle. Carbet (whose real name was Anna Marie-Magdeleine) through her niece, Dr. Yolande Marie-Magdeleine, shortly before her death in 1996. This volume, therefore, is partly the fulfilling of a trust—a promise I made to Carbet's devoted niece, who gave me access willingly and lovingly to her ninety-two-year-old aunt, that I would read and share Marie-Magdeleine Carbet's work with the world. Complementing these new stories are three previously published stories, two of which, "Le «Quimbois»" (Obeah) and "Le capitaine se marie" (The Captain Is Getting Married), were originally published in *Braves gens de la Martinique* (Fort-de-France: La Cité du Livre, 1957), a collection coauthored by "Claude et Magdelleine Carbet." The third "old" story that I have used to close this volume, "La poupée de son" (The Straw Doll), was previously published in Carbet's 1980 collection, *Contes de Tantana*.

The literature of the French Caribbean during the twentieth century has been dominated by the genres of poetry, the novel, the essay, and drama. The "conte" or short story has to a large extent been overlooked, even though many of the canonical writers, including Joseph Zobel, Bertène Juminer, have published important contributions in this genre. Moreover, the focus on the concerns of identity and on reactions to the experience of slavery and colonization have diverted attention from the exploration of the daily lives of "ordinary" Martinican folk, to the extent that the impression derived from the better-known literary representations of Martinican life is that Martinicans have little personal and private life outside of the omnipresence of colonial oppression. Consequently, the impression readers derive of the Martinican "reality" tends to be incomplete or even distorted. Carbet's political commitment to eradicate racism went hand in hand with a deep appreciation for Martinican folk and folk culture, and she sought to celebrate, validate, and immortalize this aspect of Martinique through her short stories.

The short stories written and published by Carbet are difficult to obtain, since most of them are already out of print, and none have been translated into English. In fact, so far, the only English translations available of any of Carbet's works have been my translations of some of her poems "Marie-Magdeleine Carbet," in *Through a Black Veil: Readings in French Caribbean Poetry*, and poems in *The Oxford Book of Caribbean Verse*. The bold poetic initiatives on Carbet's part that we have seen in "Transplant" and "Torment" are counterbalanced in the stories that appear in this volume and in much of her poetic and prose works by the treatment of themes that appear to be out of step with the racially charged publications of the Negritude era. The stories in this collection provide a rare perspective on the activities, sorrows, and joys of ordinary Martinican folk. The situations and characters presented in these stories provide some of the missing links of the French Caribbean social scene. These stories focus on aspects of Carbet's sensibility that were long present in her writing: a love for fantasy and for the folklore of Martinique, coupled with a profound Christian faith.

The story that I have used to open this volume, "Le «Quimbois»" ("Obeah"), in a way sets the tone for the sociocultural elements that, from Carbet's perspective, characterize Martinique—a world in which fantasy and reality converge. Loulou, a simple agricultural worker, finds himself suffering from an unnamed, unexplainable malaise. The only solution, which he is afraid even to consider, is a consultation with the Rozane, the local obeah-woman. He finally finds the courage to go to her place, and when the opportunity arises for him to steal the spell that he believes will solve his problem he does not hesitate. The narrative perspective validates with gentle irony the power of the African-derived cultural belief system and practices that dominate the daily lives of African-heritage peoples throughout the Americas, in the wake of European colonization, and take a variety of forms and designations, including roots, vaudou, candomblé, santería, obeah, and so on. In this story, as in all the others, there is no explicit reference to political or ideological questions. The focus is on the activities and interests of Martinican working-class folk, as they engage in and struggle to resolve the challenges that confront them on a day-to-day basis. "Obeah" places the reader firmly in a cultural context that is typically Caribbean and Martinican.

In "Easter Story: The Return," both the title and the subtitle of the story explain its significance and intention within Carbet's belief system. Both serve to illustrate and underscore her profound Christian faith. Also significant is the fact that "Tantana," the name by which Anna Marie-Magdeleine is affectionately called by her nieces and nephews in real life, literally appears as a character in the story, which adds a directly autobiographical element to the narrative. This autobiographical aspect is further enhanced by the insertion in the narrative of one of Tantana's (i.e., Carbet's) poems from *Comptines et chansons antillaises*, published in 1975. Thus, this story exemplifies an indissoluble fusion of reality and fiction.

Tantana, however, is not the narrator. The story, narrated in the third person, opens with an aphorism about the vagaries of chance and its indifference to the emotional desires or state of human beings. The story focuses on the love affair between Caroline and Robert, two people from different geographical and cultural locations, who produce the most beautiful baby, Anne. This child, however, turns out to be deaf-mute. Their second child, Michèle, is equally pretty. But the care and attention needed by Anne place severe strain on the family, emotionally and materially, to the point where they begin to blame each other. But they devote themselves to caring for Anne and following the directions given them by the specialists, until Anne one day speaks one hoarse word, "Daddy." After that, Anne makes rapid progress, goes to a special school, and participates in an exhibition of arts and crafts produced by the schoolchildren. One of her special guests is "Tantana." The child's amazing progress is marked by the fact that she is able to read one of Tantana's poems in a clear, well-articulated voice. The narrator interprets Anne's achievement as a miracle, as one sign of the presence and return of Christ, of the resurrection celebrated at Easter, and invites the reader, the audience, to join in this form of belief.

"Christmas Story" focuses on characteristic elements of French Caribbean cultural identity: the Creole language and the fondness for using Creole proverbs, as well as the cultural practice of killing pigs and the cooking of "pudding" (using the pig's intestines) on Saturdays. The proverb that serves as an epigraph for the story, "Every pig has his Saturday," is different in its significance from the English proverb "Every dog has his day." While the English adage is an expression of encouragement, empowerment, and hope for the lowliest of creatures, the Martinican proverb as used in this story alludes to a more complex exploration of the notion of fatality, in the context of the belief that actions bear inevitable consequences.

The story, following in the tradition of folktales, is intended to illustrate the deeper significance of the proverb. The story introduces us to a loving couple—a Martinican country woman and a European artist—who give birth to a beautiful baby, but whose existence is complicated by poverty. The critical action of the plot takes place at Christmas when the artist father, with nothing else to give at this season of giving but the gift of his talent as a painter, decides to paint a portrait of the sleeping child, which turns out to be a masterpiece, and offer that to his wife. During the following year, the couple confronts serious challenges: dire financial constraints and deterioration in the health of their child. The gravity of the situation leads them to entertain the extremely painful decision to separate. This decision would call for a division of the only two assets they possess—the child and the portrait. While they could agree that the mother should have the child, only reluctantly could the mother consider relinquishing her portrait. As they stare in tearful agony at the painting, a miracle occurs: the portrait becomes animated. This miracle impels them to fall on their knees and renew their faith in the promise of Christmas.

So what is the moral of the story? What lesson does the loving couple learn? The story offers a complex set of messages. Just as Saturday represents the accomplishment of the pig's destiny in the Caribbean cultural context, thereby giving significance and value to the pig's existence, the story insists on the necessity for faith and the possibility of miracles in human affairs.

Our third story, "The Gift," may be read as a statement about the belief system of the narrator: a belief in Christian Catholic doctrine as well as in a world of miracles and fantasy that is consistent with the reality of life in Martinique. The story establishes a link among faith (Christian faith), miracles, and fantasy, and the world of animals is used as a mechanism for emphasizing this linkage. In fact, at the heart of this story is the special relationship that exists between Tantana and animals.

The primary narrator of "The Gift" is Tantana, aunt to the interlocutor, the person to whom the storytelling is addressed. The "story" fuses reality—explicit references to the activities that we know MMC participated in—with fantasy, in the stories related by Tantana. The story moves from a conversation between aunt and niece about boxes that contain information and memories about Tantana's past to a focus on animals, triggered by a box containing information about Tantana's membership in the SPA (Society for the Protection of Animals). The focus on this box stimulates the recall of a fairy tale (Tantana specifically mentions that "fairies" form part of the story)—a Christmas story that ends with a miracle.

This story, which starts as a third-person narrative of a conversation between Tantana and her niece, moves to a first-person story, narrated by Tantana. It begins with Tantana's adoption of a little dog, bringing it back with her to Martinique and giving it the name Joy. Tantana's narrative follows Joy's adaptation to the Martinican environment, the eventual illness that threatens his existence, and his mysterious disappearance on the day he was scheduled to be put down, which coincidentally happens to be the day before Christmas Eve.

This story leads to another: the story of Mangot the cat, who had disappeared on a picnic trip and reappeared mysteriously a week later. And this story leads to yet another story—an occurrence on the Christmas following Joy's mysterious disappearance—relating the mystery of a special Christmas gift that Tantana receives in the form of another miracle dog.

The moral of the story is posed by the narrator in the form of a question: Does not Christmas assure us that miracles are possible and therefore that all that is needed is faith?

"The Captain Is Getting Married" subtly juxtaposes the competing value systems of Martinican men and women. Against the physical backdrop of the Caribbean Sea and its significance as a magnetic doorway and an almost irresistible pole of attraction to the world beyond the island, the narrative provides an exploration of the different emotional and practical preoccupations of two lovers. It poses fascinating questions on the meaning and importance of love and marriage for men and women, on the possible imbalance of their interests and values, and on possible conflictual manifestations of commitment and obsession.

"Larammée's Two Squares" adopts the form of a story within a story, in that it opens on a storytelling scene in which the first-person narrator is about to tell a story to an audience: "Now that the lights are on, I'd be happy to tell you my tale." The immediate atmosphere is one of mystery and magic: the narrator alludes to the danger of being turned into a basket if she tells the story in the daytime.

This story attempts to explain the "origin" and significance of the Martinican use of the expression "God willing" and other traditional Martinican expressions and proverbs, such as "Dog hair heals dog bite" and "Every word not good to say nor all food good to eat."

The three critical characters in the story are God, the dog Toby, and Larammée. The relationship among these three serves to explain a range of peculiarities: the fragmentation among living creatures as manifested in their different languages; the origin of conflict among people, animals, and nature; the loss of speech by animals; even the way dogs sleep and their non-verbal communication, as well as the intervention of God in human affairs.

The final story, "The Straw Doll," takes us into a world of fantasy in which all creatures, human and nonhuman, flora and fauna, are animate, invested with human characteristics and qualities. It is essentially a fable in the tradition of those attributed to Aesop and La Fontaine. The heroine is a beautiful, innocent doll stuffed with straw, named Magiquette, who lives in an enchanted forest, but later falls under the spell of an evil fairy, the primary elements of whose character are reflected in the various nicknames by which she is called by members of the forest community—Lady All-for-me, Lady Heart-of-Ice, Crocodile, or Teary-Eyes. At first Magiquette is forced to sacrifice her freedom to this evil fairy, but eventually, willingly and with tragic nobility, sacrifices her literally inner self of straw to help the one who selfishly exploited her goodness. Magiquette has to face almost certain destruction before her liberation comes from the relationship she enjoys with the members of the community of which she is a part. This is essentially a fable that extolls the virtues of kindness, charity, and friendship, one in which goodness, innocence, and purity triumph over evil, and which conveys a powerful moral lesson of unity, equality, fraternity, and above all love.

All these stories re-create and validate the Martinican tradition of storytelling, and in their fusion of fantasy and reality place Marie-Magdeleine Carbet at the center of this valorization of Martinican culture. Thus, Anna Marie-Magdeleine's identity, in the twin personas of Tantana, the narrator of folktales, and of Marie-Magdeleine Carbet, the writer, the identity that she constantly celebrates, insists on its essentially Martinican and Antillean or Caribbean nature, rather than African. This focus has immense significance. While some commentators may consider this insistence on a Caribbean-Antillean-Martinican specificity as participating in the colonial tendency to exoticize the Caribbean and thus marginalize, infantilize, and exclude Caribbean people, Carbet's choice reinforces a reality that some proponents of the need to privilege recognition of the African element in African-heritage peoples of the Caribbean find troubling. There is a school of thought among Caribbean people that the Caribbean experience, however brutal it was for African-heritage people, represents the opportunity for the development of a "new," never before experienced culture, manifested in the response and adaptation to new social, economic, racial, and linguistic realities. This adaptation results in an appropriation of the new cultural space and the development of enormous pride in belonging to the new geographical and cultural locations.

One of the most prominent twentieth-century leaders of African-consciousness movements, the Jamaican Marcus Garvey, alluded to the lack of racial consciousness among African-heritage Caribbean people and their apparent complacent acceptance of their condition as the demographic majority group in their individual territories, and their lack of willingness to change a situation that for him represented assimilation into and subordination to European colonial conditioning:

> There is great misfortune surrounding the West Indian Negro at home. It is his inability to develop a true racial consciousness in the midst of an environment that would make him master of the situation. He is unable to develop this racial consciousness because of the superior intellectual and political manoeuvres of those who control his destiny. There is nothing done to him in the West Indies in the way of racial demonstration, as to make him feel positively hurt, to the extent of stirring his racial consciousness, but everything is done hypocritically

to let him believe everything else but that he is a Negro; and so he has developed a peculiar psychology that seems difficult to explain, because in the West Indies he is more white than he is black, hence his inability to develop truly on racial lines, even though he lives in the midst of golden opportunities. ("The West Indian Negro," *The Blackman* [May/June 1934])

Even Carbet's compatriot and friend Paulette Nardal, in her essay "Awakening of Race Consciousness," expressed a similar view of Caribbean people and even alluded to continental Africans as "retarded brothers":

We are fully conscious of our debts to the Latin culture and we have no intention of discarding it in order to promote I know not what return to ignorance. Without it we would have never become conscious of our real selves. But we want to go beyond this culture, in order to give to our brethren, with the help of the white scientists and friends of the Negroes, the pride of being the members of a race which is perhaps the oldest in the world. Once informed of the civilisation, they will no longer despair of the future of their own race, a part of which seems at the present time to be delayed in evolution. They will tender to their retarded brothers a helping hand and endeavour to understand and love them better. ("Éveil de la conscience de race/Awakening of Race Consciousness," *La Revue du Monde Noir/The Review of the Black World* 6 [April 1932]: 31)

Carbet belongs, therefore, to the group of Antilleans who, like Paulette Nardal, are grateful for the benefits of French and European civilization and culture. Her education, her exposure to and respect for French culture do not, however, cause her to become alienated from her Martinican people and culture. She is well aware of the deleterious effect of racism. She is motivated by a profound admiration for the Martinican culture with which she identifies, and which she considers as a fundamental aspect of her personal identity as a Martinican. It is this culture to which she pays tribute, and which she seeks to preserve and even immortalize in her works. This motivation explains why she becomes involved in so many different forms of cultural expression: songs, recipes, plays, short stories, essays, novels, and poetry.

Carbet, consequently, attaches considerable value to the Martinican and Caribbean oral tradition through which cultural knowledge is transmitted. For this reason, she devotes a lot of attention to proverbs, to the Creole language, and to storytelling.

The convergence of Christian faith—an undeniable manifestation of European colonization—and the realm of the magical in these stories underscores a peculiarity of the Caribbean reaction to the experience of being colonized. While it is beyond dispute that the colonizing experience has in its essence been oppressive and violent, resulting in extreme dehumanization of both colonizer and colonized, the imposition of religious and linguistic practices as pathways to (European) civilization, added to the direct oppression in the form of forced labor and inhuman punishments, and indoctrination into a self-concept of inferiority—based on the unchangeable condition of skin color considered as morally reprehensible (associated with evil within the Christian belief system) as well as esthetically unacceptable (an ineradicable "ugliness" of such bodily features as breadth of nose, texture of hair, and color of skin)—yet African-heritage Caribbean people over the centuries have been able to find hope, solace, and inspiration, paradoxically, in the very religion that was used to justify their humiliation, denigration, oppression, and enslavement.

The attachment that African-heritage people throughout the Americas display to a variety of adaptations and syncretizations of Christian beliefs and rituals suggests that a profound spirituality is a characteristic of these people. Part of the creativity of African-heritage people in the Caribbean and Americas has been the use of whatever tools were available to aid in survival and growth. Thus, Christian ritual and faith could be adapted and adopted to complement existing, however fragmentary, folk beliefs transmitted orally through proverbs and other sayings, as well as through stories.

In all societies and cultures, people have apparently found observed material reality insufficient to explain the complexities of other sensed immaterialities. This perceived insufficiency has always produced recourse to fantasy. The mixing of faith and fantasy, therefore, in these stories by Carbet is in line with traditional strategies of resistance, survival, and knowledge transmission. The convergence of fantasy and reality in the lives of colonized peoples in the Americas has manifested itself artistically in what has been called variously Marvelous or Magical Realism. In this representation of the paradox of life in the colonized societies of the "New World," ancient beliefs and ways of perceiving exist hand in hand and have to be reconciled with a reality that is often harsh and painful. The human need for meaning and beauty seeks reconciliation between the conflicting realities, and expresses itself artistically in the form of magical realism. Carbet's stories that follow belong to this realm of expression in which what some might consider fantasy is integrated into daily life, and a belief in the miraculous is a sine qua non for adapting to the challenges of a lived reality made immeasurably more challenging, more difficult to reconcile, in the wake of European enslavement, colonization, exploitation, and continuous devaluation of African-heritage peoples and cultures.

"Obeah" and
Other Martinican Stories

Le «Quimbois»

Le vent sauvage des tropiques accourt du large. Nourri d'embruns, salé, gueulard, fleurant la marée, il fouaille les criques, s'acharne sur les cocotiers qu'il crible de volées de sable. Puis il galope vers les mornes.

Dans l'herbe des savanes, sur les talus des chemins, il pleut des fruits mûrs. Couleurs et parfums confondus, les corolles volent.

Cinq heures. Au loin, sur une cadence de biguine, les cloches appellent les fidèles. Dans les palmiers les merles sifflent leur «prière matinale». Tandis qu'en chute bigarrée la volaille quitte les citronniers, le ciel rosit. Ni meilleur, ni pire que les autres, voici un jour nouveau. Mais jouir de l'air et du soleil tout neufs, vivre et lutter encore aujourd'hui semble dépasser les forces de Loulou. L'habitude l'arrache de sa couche. Mais autour de sa case, il traînaille, le geste lent. Pourtant, l'ouvrage attend. Il lui faut partir.

Enfin, son café noir avalé, Loulou, coutelas en main et houe sur l'épaule, s'en va berçant sa peine d'une complainte:

«Moin planté pensées
C'est soucis moin récolté . . .»

Au fait quels soucis l'accablent? Autrefois, fier de sa force, il faisait orgueilleusement saillir les muscles sous son cuir noir, luisant au soleil. Et son rire heureux résonnait à tout propos. Maintenant le jeune nègre semble, dos rond, lèvres serrées, regard terni, indifférent à tout.

Ainsi l'appel du voisin retentit par trois fois par-dessus la haie: «O . . . O Loulou ô . . . ô! qui nove?»

En vain. Une secousse de l'autre le réveillant, il répond mollement, une angoisse dans la voix. L'espace d'une seconde, Asson hésite. Il pense au vieux dicton «Zaffai cabrite pas zaffai mouton» et puis, au diable la sagesse, il entreprend de confesser Loulou. Mais quel nom donner au mal qui le ronge? Loulou n'a rien de précis. Peut-être, un mauvais sort? On a dû lui jeter un sort! Mais qui? Asson se penche à son oreille.

—Céline, Maïotte, Ti-Thé? Tu les courtisais en même temps. L'une d'elles, pour se venger, t'aura sans doute «piaillé».

Consterné, le pauvre Loulou baisse la tête. Il revoit le regard humide de l'une; la bouche provocante de l'autre; et de la troisième, la démarche houleuse.

—...Consulter Rozane, murmure Asson...

Rozane! ! ! Loulou se signe. Approcher cette sorcière, il n'osera jamais!

—On dit qu'elle vit comme un monstre, balbutie Loulou. On dit...

—On dit surtout qu'elle réussit toujours! Rappelle-toi Ti-Dore, mon propre cousin qu'elle a guéri d'un seul coup! Et le mariage de Souloune, elle ne l'a pas fait le mariage de Souloune? Tu crois que ce beau Monsieur de la ville aurait reconnu ses petits et l'aurait épousée si la vieille Zane n'y avait donné un coup de pouce?

Mal convaincu, Loulou résiste encore. Le voudrait-il qu'il ne pourrait consulter Rozane. Elle a tiré bien des gens d'affaire, soit. Mais à quel prix? Chacun de ses sortilèges coûte une fortune.

—Allons, pas tant que ça, grogne Asson. Tes coqs de combat valent gros. Tu sais bien qu'en les vendant tous les deux tu pourrais te payer l'aide de la sorcière. Au fond, tu as peur...

Pris pour un capon? Jamais! C'est dit. Loulou ira trouver la vieille.

Un soir il enferme dans une bourse de cotonnade les billets crasseux reçus en échange de ses précieuses bêtes de race. Vêtu de son meilleur pantalon, de sa chemise rose, la plus belle, il tire derrière lui la porte de sa case. En route! Dieu lui viendra en aide! N'a-t-il pas accroché deux nouvelles médailles d'aluminium à son scapulaire de bon chrétien? Oui, Dieu le protégera, même sur ce chemin qui conduit à la demeure de la sorcière. N'arrive jamais que ce qu'Il veut. S'Il permet qu'on «piaille» un homme innocent, il doit pareillement permettre que la victime se défende. Sinon, Il ne serait ni juste ni bon!

Par la nuit sans lune des formes silencieuses frôlent les buissons. Elles longent les champs de canne à sucre dont bruissent, comme une eau légère, les flèches soyeuses. Elles surgissent, s'éloignent, s'amassent et se défont. La piste serpente au bord d'un talus. Elle traverse la voie ferrée conduisant à l'usine proche, puis soudain, elle grimpe la rampe d'une côte assez dure, pour dominer ensuite une sorte de gouffre. Loulou avance, l'oreille bourdonnante de la voix des insectes nocturnes, des soupirs du feuillage, et surtout de la clameur de l'océan, à chaque tournant plus sensible. Les histoires étranges contées aux veillées des morts lui reviennent en mémoire. On les écoute en tremblant délicieusement, le punch ou le café noir en main. Ici, en cette randonnée solitaire, leur souvenir fait frissonner.

Tous l'assurent. Si d'aventure sur le coup de minuit des ailes velues battent aux fenêtres; si une infernale cavalcade sème l'épouvante au village; si des feux sautent de l'un à l'autre des pitons et des mornes ne cherchez pas qui mène le train, c'est Rozane!

Le pauvre Loulou sent croître son malaise. Il se gourmande et se parle et s'encourage à la mode nègre:

—Courage, Loulou, quimbé fô, nèg. Ouè misè pas mô!

D'ailleurs, voici la dernière étape. Le voyageur évite un groupe de pêcheurs nocturnes. Quelques hommes s'agitent en effet à la lueur de «serbis» fumeux; fouillant la vase de leurs bâtons, ils cherchent des crabes de terre. Loulou dépasse une crique où dorment les gommiers hissés sur leurs rondins. Il arrive. Il est arrivé. Voici, au bout d'une sente la «chapelle» qui indique l'entrée de la case. Un lampion flotte sur un doigt d'huile dans un verre d'eau. La flamme de la veilleuse vacille au vent. Le doigt pointé vers le cœur, un «bon Dieu» de plâtre préside aux offrandes des chalands . . .

Loulou se sèche le front où perle une sueur glacée. Il ne peut plus reculer. La voici la case de Zane. Le Chef Soucliant, Zane «Maman Quimbois!». Basse, accroupie, cul dans la vase, étayée de pilotis d'un côté, la case a l'air d'une bête se dressant sur ses pattes de devant. Les lames en lèchent presque le seuil. Une avare clarté filtre des cloisons mal jointes. Loulou approche, tellement intrigué qu'il en oublie sa peur.

Horreur! Epouvante! Sa tignasse crépue se hérisse!

La pièce est sinistre, presque nue. D'un tas de haillons, posé à même le plancher, émerge une tête hideuse et qui n'a plus rien d'humain. Les yeux, barrés de taie blanche, certainement privés de regard, n'ont même plus de cils . . . A la place du nez, deux grands trous noirs . . . dans un fouillis de rides, une fente, taillée de travers, la bouche . . .

C'est «ça» Zane la toute-puissante, Zane la quimboiseuse, la sorcière, dont la seule pensée fait trembler tant de gens! Un épouvantail, ni plus, ni moins. Loulou en rirait se le spectacle n'était si abject.

Il pourrait entrer là, et s'emparer de force de tous les sortilèges, et de ce déchet même, au besoin!

Pour l'instant, deux clientes, occupent la place. Deux femmes, deux dames, plus exactement, l'une très jeune et qui a l'air égaré, l'autre assez âgée, le désespoir sur la face.

—Mère et fille . . . dans la peine, depuis longtemps . . . laisse tomber Rozane. Prenez les cartes, sur la table. Mêlez. Coupez. Passez-les moi, ordonne-t-elle.

Trois têtes se penchent sur le jeu étalé sur le parquet.

Rozane bougonne des mots sans suite, dans un silence épais. Brusquement elle semble se mettre en colère.

—Parlez! mais parlez donc! ou alors, allez-vous en!

La voix, stridente, ténue, cingle comme des lianes empoisonnées.

Entre les plis de sa robe blanche, la plus jeune des femmes s'affaisse soudain. La mère blêmit encore et se raidit. Alors, apparemment radoucie, la sorcière parle.

—Je n'ai pas besoin des cartes pour y voir clair. Un jour, votre fille a respiré un bouquet de roses rouges offert par une inconnue. Elle était fiancée, n'est-ce pas? Une rivale se vengeait . . . car du coup, votre fille a perdu la raison. Depuis, des années ont passé. Il fallait venir plus tôt. J'essaierai de vous trouver un remède, mais c'est tard!

Des minutes passent, lentes comme des heures. Enfin, un bras sorti du tas de haillons tend un minuscule paquet vers la mère éplorée.

Déjà les femmes s'éloignent. Loulou sort de l'ombre. Il demeure indécis. Un grand cri. Puis une galopade! Prise de peur sans doute la malade s'est mise à courir. Sa mère la poursuit en toute hâte.

Sur le sable humide aux pieds de Loulou gît le mystérieux paquet. Le sortilège qui rend l'équilibre, le «charme» qui neutralise les vengeances, le bouclier, le porte-bonheur, il le tient, il l'a. Bon Saint Michel! Est-ce possible! Il l'a le sortilège! Et pour rien! sans avoir affronté la vieille sorcière, sans avoir gaspillé le prix de ses coqs!

Loulou se sauve à toutes jambes. Il court, et court encore, la main sur le cœur, pour en contenir les battements. Quant à sa conscience, pas trop tranquille, un dicton lui impose le calme: «Ça qui à tè, c'est à chiens!» «Aux chiens, ce qui gît sur le sol!»

Désormais sauvé, Loulou se sent des ailes. Il saute les ravines, grimpe à l'assaut des mornes. Parvenu en haut de la falaise, il s'arrête enfin, hors d'haleine. Alors il desserre les doigts et contemple son trésor. Un cheval de mer, ficelé dans la soie! Le roi des quimbois! le quimbois tout puissant, le quimbois par excellence!

Loulou jubile! Il se signe! Il rit, pleure, éclate en chanson!

«La rue déyè là, té ni en vieu case . . .
Déyè case la té ni en pié piment
Adan case-la té ni en ti vieu femme . . .
Chaleu vieux madamm-là, brulé pié pimen-à.»

A-t-il dansé de joie? Une roche a-t-elle cédé sous son pas? Qui jamais le saura? Voici que du haut de la falaise dévalent pêle-mêle du gravât, des pierres . . . un pantin désarticulé . . .

Dans la campagne encore déserte l'aube qui se lève demeure calme et sereine. Nulle oreille n'a recueilli le cri du jeune imprudent. Et pourtant, tassée sur son plancher crasseux, une boule d'argile aux doigts, Zane la sorcière lui fait écho d'un ricanement sec.

Obeah

THE WILD WIND OF THE TROPICS RUSHES INLAND FROM THE OPEN SEA.
Fed with spray, salty, blustering, and perfuming the tide, it lashes coves and
harasses coconut trees, riddling them with volleys of sand, then gallops
towards the hills.

Ripe fruits rain down on the grassy savannas and on the slopes of the
roadways. Flower petals fly about, a mix of colors and fragrances.

It's five o'clock. In the distance, church bells chiming to the rhythm
of a biguine summon the faithful. In the palm trees blackbirds chirp their
"morning prayer." The sky turns rosy as a multicolored flock of fowls fall
out of the lemon trees. Here is a new day, no better or worse than any other.
But it seems to be beyond Loulou's strength today to enjoy the brand new
air and sun, to live and fight again. Habit drags him from his bed. But he
dawdles around his hut, moving very slowly. Yet, work is waiting. He has to
leave.

At last, Loulou swallows his black coffee and goes off, with cutlass in
hand and hoe on shoulder, singing a lament to soothe his pain:

Thoughts me sow
But worries me reap . . .

So what are his major worries? In the good old days, proud of his
strength, he used to show off the muscles rippling under his black hide,
glistening in the sun. And his happy laugh would boom out constantly.
Now the young Negro, his back bent, his lips tight, doesn't seem interested
in anything.

A call from his neighbor rings out three times over the hedge: "O . . . O Loulou, wha's up?"

No use. Jolted awake by his neighbor's shout, Loulou answers feebly, with anguish in his voice. Asson hesitates for just a second. He is thinking about the old saying "Goat business is not sheep business." And then, not listening to common sense, he starts drawing the truth out of Loulou. But how to describe the pain that is eating away at him? Loulou can't find a word for it. A curse, perhaps? Somebody must have worked obeah on him! But who? Asson leans over into his ear: "Celine, Maiotte, Ti—Thé? You were courting all of them at the same time. One of them, for revenge, has probably worked obeah on you."

Appalled, poor Loulou bows his head. He remembers the misty eyes of one of those women, the provocative mouth of another, and the third with a walk that whipped up a storm.

"Go see Rozane," Asson whispers . . .

"Rozane!!!" Loulou makes the sign of the cross. He would never dare approach that obeah-woman!

"They say she lives like a monster," Loulou stammers. "They say . . ."

"They say particularly that she always succeeds! Remember Ti-Dore, my own cousin that she cured immediately! And Souloune's marriage. Didn't she bring off Souloune's marriage? You think that that fine city gent would have recognized his children and married her if old Zane hadn't put her finger in the pie?"

Loulou is not completely convinced and still resists. He would really prefer not to have to consult Rozane. She really helped a lot of people, agreed. But at what cost? Each of her spells cost a fortune.

"Come on, not that much," Asson grumbles. "Your fighting cocks are worth a lot. You know that if you sell both of them you could pay for the obeah-woman's services. But basically you're afraid . . ."

To be taken for a coward? Never! That's it. Loulou will go find the old woman.

One evening he puts the filthy bills he had received in exchange for his precious bloodstock in a cotton purse. He dresses in his best trousers and his pink shirt, the most beautiful one he has, and pulls the door of his hut shut behind him. Off he goes! God will help him! Did he not pin two new aluminum medals to his chest like a good Christian? Yes, God will protect him, even on this path leading to the obeah-woman's home. Only what God wants will happen. If he allows an innocent man to have obeah worked on him, he must similarly allow the victim to defend himself. Otherwise, God could not be either fair or good!

Silent forms brush against the bushes in the moonless night. They run alongside the sugar cane fields whose silky arrows rustle like light water. They appear suddenly, form clusters, and then separate. The trail winds on the edge of a slope. It crosses the railway leading to the nearby factory, suddenly climbs the slope of a rather harsh hillside, and then overlooks a kind of abyss. Loulou moves forward, his ears buzzing with the voices of the nocturnal insects, the sighs of the foliage, and especially the clamor of the ocean, which becomes more perceptible at every bend. He now remembers the strange stories that are told at wakes. They are listened to in trembling delight, with rum punch or black coffee in hand. Here, on this solitary hike, the memories of these stories make him shiver.

They all reach the same conclusion. If by chance on the stroke of midnight hairy wings beat at windows; if a hellish cavalcade sows terror in the village; if fires jump from peak to peak and from hill to hill—you don't have to ask who is responsible, it's Rozane!

Poor Loulou feels his uneasiness grow. He rebukes himself, talks to himself, and encourages himself as black countryfolk do:

"Have no fear, Loulou, be strong, man. What don't kill you makes you stronger!"

Anyway, this is the last stage. Loulou walks around a group of night fishermen. Some men are moving about in the smoky glow of straw torches. They rummage in the mud with their sticks, looking for land crabs. Loulou passes a cove where the little fishing boats are sleeping hoisted on their logs. He is almost there. He has arrived. Here at the end of a path is the "chapel" that marks the entrance to the hut. A lantern is floating on a drop of oil in a water glass. The flame of the night-light flickers in the wind. A plaster Jesus, with his finger pointed toward his heart, presides over the offertory from the barges . . .

Loulou dries the beads of icy sweat on his forehead. He cannot go back now. Here is Zane's hut. The Chief of the Sorcerers, Zane, "Mama Obeah!"

The hut, low, crouched, its backside in the mud, propped up by stilts on one side, looks like an animal rearing up on its front legs. The waves almost wash up against its doorway. A miserly glow of light filters through badly assembled partitions. Loulou draws closer, so intrigued that he forgets his fear.

Horror! Terror! His kinky hair stands on end!

The room is sinister, almost completely bare. A hideous head that has nothing human about it emerges from a heap of rags positioned right down on the floor. The eyes, an opaque white film blocking them out, are definitely sightless, and have even lost their lids . . . Instead of a nose, there are two large black holes . . . and, in a jumble of wrinkles, there is a slit, cut crosswise, the mouth . . .

That's the Almighty Zane, Zane the "obeah-woman," the witch, the very thought of whom causes so many people to tremble! A scarecrow, no more, no less. Loulou would have laughed if the sight of her was not so pitiful.

He could get in there and grab all the spells by force, and even this piece of trash, if he wanted to!

At the moment, there are two clients in the room. Two women, or to be more precise, two ladies, a very young one looking lost, and the other one fairly old, with despair in her face.

"Mother and daughter . . . suffering, for a long time now . . ." Rozane mutters. "Take the cards on the table. Shuffle them. Cut. Pass them to me," she orders.

Three heads bend over the deck spread out on the floor.

In a thick silence, Rozane grumbles some disjointed words. Suddenly she seems to get angry:

"Speak! Go on, speak! or go away!"

Her voice, shrill and reedy, stings like a poisoned vine.

The younger woman suddenly collapses between the folds of her white dress. The mother turns pale and stiffens. Then the obeah-woman, apparently back to her softer self again, speaks:

"I don't need the cards to see what's been going on. One day, your daughter smelled a bouquet of red roses given to her by somebody she didn't know. She was engaged to be married, wasn't she? A rival took revenge . . .

and as a result, your daughter lost her mind. Since then, years have passed. You should have come sooner. I will try to find a cure for you, but it is already late!"

Minutes pass, as slow as hours. Finally, an arm emerges from the heap of rags and hands a tiny package to the tearful mother.

The women are already moving off. Loulou comes out of the shadows. He remains undecided.

There is a loud cry, then a mad rush! The sick young woman, overcome by fear no doubt, sets off running. Her mother chases after her as fast as possible.

On the wet sand at Loulou's feet lies the mysterious package. He is holding it; he has it—the magic spell that restores balance, the "charm" that neutralizes acts of revenge, the shield, the lucky charm. Blessed Saint Michael! Is it possible? He has the spell! And for nothing! Without having to face the old witch, without having to waste what he got for his cocks!

Loulou takes off as fast as his legs will take him. He runs on and on, his hand on his heart, as if to hold its beating in check. As far as his conscience is concerned, which is not too quiet, an old saying brings him calm: "Whuh pun de groung is dog wun" or "What's on the ground belongs to the dogs!"

Now that he's been saved, Loulou feels as if he has wings. He jumps over gullies, charges over hills. When he reaches the top of the cliff, he finally stops, out of breath. Then he opens his fingers and looks at his treasure. A sea horse, tied up in a silk cloth! The king of the obeah charms! The all-powerful obeah charm, the grandmaster of obeah charms!

Loulou is in ecstasy! He makes the sign of the cross! He laughs, weeps, breaks out in song!

> In the street in the back was an old house
> Behind the house was a hot pepper tree
> In the house was an old woman
> She was so hot she killed the pepper tree.

Did he dance with joy? Did a rock give way under his feet? Who will ever know? All we know is that from the top of the cliff rubble and rocks rain down . . . a puppet with its limbs torn off . . .

In the still deserted countryside, dawn that is rising remains calm and serene. No ear heard the cry of the foolhardy young man. However, you could hear the echo of a dry cackle from Zane the obeah-woman, slumped on the filthy floor, a ball of clay in her fingers.

Conte de Pâques

Le Retour

Le râteau du croupier disperse, rassemble les jetons sur le tapis vert. Au gré du hasard qui n'a cure du drame des joueurs.

De même, insoucieux des questions secondaires de race et d'origine, le sort fantaisiste a conduit et mis en présence entre les murs de Paris—ce creuset des peuples—deux jeunes gens, Caroline et Robert.

Alors qu'elle est «montée» de sa province méridionale, lui, a bel et bien traversé l'Atlantique. A la rencontre l'un de l'autre, sans s'en douter.

Se découvrir, s'aimer, fonder un foyer . . . ils s'y sont décidés, confiants. Avec raison, puisque les voici penchés sur un berceau où sourit le plus beau bébé du monde.

De proportions parfaites. Teint d'ambre velouté des sapotilles mûries au soleil. Duvet noir mousseux, frisé autour des oreilles, deux orchidées brunes. La bouche, les mains, les pieds, des coquillages ouvragés et tendres.

Une réussite, ce fruit de leurs amours, Anne, éveillée déjà, les yeux particulièrement expressifs. Des yeux, au fait, un peu inquiétants. Parce que, en alternance, trop vifs, ou pas assez.

De sang froid, l'observateur attentif s'en aperçoit, à la longue. Tantôt le regard de l'enfant, calme, lointain, semble tourné vers l'intérieur. Tantôt il s'allume et brûle d'un feu intense. Exceptionnel. Il y a quelque chose d'insolite. Inconsciemment d'abord, ensuite avec prudence, Caroline et Robert, chacun de son côté, épient les réactions de l'enfant. Gardant chacun, des impressions par devers soi.

De plus en plus nettement, ils s'aperçoivent que le bébé paraît indifférent au bruit. Et, jusqu'au son de leurs voix. Ils n'osent pas se l'avouer. Se refusent tacitement à l'admettre.

Passent les jours, les semaines. Et vont croissantes la circonspection, la crainte qui se font angoisse au cœur des jeunes parents.

Il faut bien se rendre à l'évidence. D'ailleurs, le médecin le confirme après examen, les jolies orchidées sont creuses. L'enfant est atteinte de surdité.

Lorsque vient au monde un second bébé, Michèle, poupée aux pupilles vertes, aussi potelée, aussi jolie que son aînée, le couple lui fait fête. Mais il ne peut plus mettre en doute la disgrâce d'Anne, condamnée de naissance au silence total, au cruel isolement des sourds-muets.

—«Votre présence constante, une attention, des soins de toutes les heures, peuvent énormément pour elle» affirment les spécialistes à Caroline.

Rester auprès de sa fille? S'appliquer à guetter l'éclosion de sa sensibilité, l'éveil de son esprit . . . améliorer pour elle contact et communication avec autrui? La jeune maman ne rêve que de s'y consacrer! Mais comment faire? Comment renoncer à son salaire mensuel sans détruire l'équilibre du budget familial? Envisager les frais du coûteux traitement nécessaire à Anne alors que les charges déjà lourdes s'aggravent d'une nouvelle naissance?

Chaque jour plus soucieuse, Caroline devient de plus en plus taciturne. Et Robert aussi s'enferme dans un silence obscur. A quel saint se vouer? Comment augmenter ses revenus? Gagner plus pour permettre à Caroline de se libérer du bureau, de rester auprès de l'enfant? Ah! S'assurer les services des meilleurs spécialistes! Procurer les soins les plus éclairés, les plus efficaces à la fillette!

L'homme se gourmande en secret. Il s'accuse d'incapacité. Se torture la conscience.

—On parle de l'influence de la mère sur l'enfant pendant la grossesse. Le climat affectif du foyer serait très important. Il déterminerait pratiquement le fonctionnement du système nerveux . . . Se répète Robert qui s'interroge: «Ai-je été le mari qu'il fallait à Caroline? Ai-je su créer autour de ma femme l'atmosphère propice à une parfaite gestation . . . l'ambiance de sérénité, de joie, indispensable à son heureux épanouissement . . . les conditions susceptibles d'assurer le maximum de chance à notre enfant?»

Robert tâche de se remettre en mémoire les menus faits de leur vie pendant la période critique. Des affrontements? Des heurts entre se femme et lui? Il ne s'en souvient pas. Sans doute, des riens, des brouilles! Jamais de scènes sérieuses. Des brouilles pour rire, aboutissant chacune à de délicieux rapprochements. Non . . . aucun différend, entre eux.

Mais, se dit le mari, avec l'entourage? N'ont manqué ni sujets de discussions d'incompréhensions à écarter . . . ni menaces de discorde à désamorcer. Que de questions déplacées à esquiver! d'erreurs à regretter, de maladresses à excuser!

—«Dis donc, Robert, qu'est-ce qu'elle a dû consommer comme café, madame ta mère!» ou encore:

—«Tu as de la chance, vieux! Si tu négliges ton bain au moins, ça ne se voit pas!»

Que de réflexions du genre «trait d'esprit . . . bon mot» ont-ils endurées au début de leur mariage, au cours de rencontres dans un milieu, entre gens en mal de tact ou d'informations!

En aparté les jeunes époux en riaient presque toujours. Aujourd'hui, Robert se ronge le sang. Caroline, tourmentée, ne se confie plus guère. Leurs propos tournent parfois à l'aigre. Entre eux s'installe de plus en plus pesant, chargé d'amertume, le silence.

—«A quoi penses-tu,» questionne dix fois le jour Robert qui finit par lancer tout de go, à propos d'une vétille:

—«Dis-le! Avoue-le que tu regrettes ton catastrophique essai de café au lait!»

Bouleversée, Caroline n'en croit pas ses oreilles! C'est donc là ce qui alimente les interminables réflexions de Robert? C'est là ce qui explique son très évident défaut de conscience en soi, le doute croissant qui l'empoisonne?

Voici qu'après la mère si profondément éprouvée, l'épouse vient à être blessée à son tour en Caroline.

Devant le péril qui menace son foyer la jeune femme fait litière de sa propre peine. Elle décide de se battre. Sur tous les fronts.

Il lui faut force et courage renouvelés.

Faire face. D'abord, sacrifier le bureau. Se contenter de la solde d'ingénieur de Robert. Réaliser des prouesses d'ordre et d'économie. Pour maintenir la marche de la maison. Réduire sans retard les dépenses. Remercier la femme de ménage. Renoncer à toute aide extérieure. Se mettre au fourneau, à la lessive.

Surtout, surtout! se recommande Caroline, ne jamais m'éloigner d'Anne.

Veiller sur elle! Pour rien au monde ne négliger ses soins. Ne laisser refroidir mon zèle ni fléchir mon attention. Il faudra associer Anne à notre activité, à toutes nos conversations, et, selon les conseils de l'orthophoniste, lui parler toujours en me plaçant face à face, les yeux dans les siens.

—«Qu'elle suive le jeu des lèvres et le mouvement de la langue. Qu'elle en étudie la position et le rôle du palais» a-t-il dit. Précisant que non seulement Anne ait à déchiffrer et saisir le mécanisme musculaire mais qu'elle parvienne à le reproduire.

—«Sa bouche, patiente, doit tracer les contours des sons . . . son regard aigu les photographier, afin qu'elle affecte forme, couleur, signification aux mots, en dépit de son oreille déficiente.»

En tant s'applique la mère, docile aux instructions si exigeantes soient-elles, tant s'évertue Caroline persévérante, infatigable que vient enfin le succès!

Un premier mot, un cri râpant au passage les cordes vocales tendues—un cri rauque mais perceptible, un nom jaillit des lèvres de la petite fille: Papa!

Baume et douceur au cœur de Robert! Du coup, lui revient flux de courage et d'énergie. Le voici qui participe avec constance, efficacité aux exercices d'élocution. Il ne s'adresse plus à Anne qu'en articulant soigneusement. A la manière de Caroline, détachant les syllabes une à une, il les projette comme balles hors de ses lèvres laborieuses.

Anne progresse rapidement. Petit à petit se multiplient les mots brefs composés d'une ou deux syllabes dont elle parvient à se servir.

Le sens de l'observation particulièrement développé, elle saisit plus vite que les autres les intentions du discours, d'après l'expression du visage.

Echanges, contacts, discussions avec elle deviennent moins malaisés. Pour la féliciter on dit d'elle volontiers qu'elle grandit «en force, en sagesse» comme de l'enfant Jésus. On pourrait ajouter: en beauté, car bien mise, soignée, soigneuse, souriante, elle est très agréable. Hormis l'acuité de son regard perçant plus rien de l'aspect ne la distingue de n'importe quelle fillette heureuse de son âge.

Jusque là peu ou prou empressée à manier le volant de la voiture, Caroline, profitant de son séjour à la maison, revoit le code de la route, se plait à s'exercer, obtient son permis de conduire en un temps record.

Bientôt c'est elle qui de leur banlieue des Hauts de Seine dépose et reprend chaque jour Michèle à son école et Robert au laboratoire.

Anne les accompagne. Sur le chemin du retour, elle fait halte avec sa mère au marché, à l'épicerie ou dans une quelconque boutique, selon les nécessités du moment. La fillette enregistre des mots nouveaux.

De retour à la maison commencent les séances de travail, en commentaire des «leçons de choses» acquises en route. Anne ni Caroline ne laissent perdre occasion ni temps. Leurs efforts ne se démentent pas. L'orthophoniste se déclare satisfait.

—«On pourrait lui cacher derrière l'oreille ce petit bouton à peine gênant propose t-il un matin. Perdu dans la masse de la chevelure, il ne se verra pas.»

Anne accepte de bon cœur la pose de l'appareil que dissimulent ses boucles. Elle s'y habitue très vite. Et Michèle qui elle aussi embellit et grandit prend sa part du souci familial: aider Anne, seconder ses parents. Elle passe tous ses loisirs auprès de sa sœur. Jeux, rires, parties de toutes sortes leur sont communes. Contestations, disputes aussi s'élèvent entre elles. Pour le plus grand bien de l'aînée qui y trouve stimulation.

A force de recherches Robert et Caroline découvrent dans le quinzième arrondissement un excellent externat pour enfants «mal entendant». Désormais, au cours du pèlerinage matinal Caroline se sépare de son aînée comme de son mari et de Michèle.

Le milieu scolaire se révèle extrêmement profitable à Anne. Elle s'y fait de très sympathiques relations. N'empêche qu'elle apprécie encore d'avantage l'amitié de sa petite sœur.

Aux vacances à la mer, à la montagne, les deux fillettes ne se quittent pas. Elles font partie des mêmes équipes sportives. Attentive, appliquée, moins étourdie, Anne excelle à la nage, l'été, comme au ski sur les pistes de neiges, l'hiver.

Lorsque les échanges avec autrui s'avèrent difficiles, ce qui est rare, Michèle intervient, aide discrètement sa sœur.

Vue de l'extérieur, leur vie est pratiquement normale. A huit ans Michèle suit le Cours Préparatoire II. Anne qui bientôt passe en sixième tient place honorable à l'institution de la rue des Favorites. D'ailleurs, ce printemps, la Direction y organise une vente de charité.

Aux très nombreux comptoirs sont exposés les travaux presque exclusivement exécutés par les élèves. Des tableaux composés, encadrés par les soins des enfants, aux menus ouvrages de lingerie, toute l'exposition témoigne de leur adresse et de leur application.

Les garçons ont surtout travaillé le carton, l'argile, le bois, le verre et même les métaux. Les filles sont responsables de mille réalisations, très variées. Broderies, dentelles, fil, laine crochetés, tricotés, tissés. En plus du pinceau, du métier à tapisser, à filer, elles ont manipulé osier souple, perles de verre, pâte à modeler, presse à relier.

Quand aux mamans elles ont rivalisé de générosité. Au buffet, rangés sur de grands plateaux, des amas de petits fours, de sandwiches, de tartes, de galettes, tentent les gourmets.

Jouant aux maîtres de maison, les élèves les plus expérimentés accueillent les visiteurs, les accompagnent, en hôtes conscients de leurs devoirs.

Plus que jamais avenante, rayonnante en sa robe d'organdi rose à volants, Anne fait des honneurs de la maison. Parmi les grandes s'il vous plaît!

C'est qu'elle a été admise à la communion solennelle cette année! La voici qui conduit au long des couloirs une de ses invitées personnelles. Une vieille dame amie de sa famille. Une vieille dame qui est un peu son homonyme puisqu'elle est baptisée «Tantana» par la grâce d'une kyrielle de jeunes amis, filleuls et neveux d'élection, dont Anne, naturellement.

La main dans la main de son guide élégant et résolu, la vieille dame traverse les salles. L'enfant ne s'arrête ni devant les croquis dont les couleurs pavoisent les murs, ni au comptoirs des victuailles où l'on a peine à se faire servir au sein de la bousculade.

Anne brûle également le stand de la pêche miraculeuse. Là, deux adolescents, lignes en main, s'escriment à saisir un butin inaccessible.

La layette non plus ne lui semble intéressante. Anne va droit à une salle déserte à l'heure de déjeuner: la librairie. Trois tables disposées en arc de cercle, couvertes de livres d'images.

D'un geste sûr l'enfant s'empare d'un volume à couverture plastifiée, rouge où s'épanouissent le sourire et le regard d'un enfant noir. Au dessus de la photo s'étale en grosse lettres le titre du livre: «Comptines et Chansons Antillaises».

Un instant immobile Anne tient les yeux fermés, comme si elle se recueille. Puis elle ouvre le livre et, repérant une page, le plus naturellement du monde elle prononce:

—«L'arc-en-ciel. Je le sais Tantana ton poème. Ecoute. Ecoute un peu, je vais te le lire.»

La vieille dame en a le souffle coupé. Elle s'appuie contre le mur. Elle s'appuie pour ne pas s'effondrer. Pour ne pas fléchir les genoux. Pour ne pas tomber à genoux!

Contenant le cri qui lui monte aux lèvres, elle s'enfonce le poing dans la bouche.

Anne a parlé . . . Anne parle. Sans peine. Couramment. Anne s'exprime de la voix, de la bouche, non plus des mains. Allègrement. Légèrement. Comme vous, comme moi, Anne se fait entendre. Elle s'entend parler! Elle contrôle sa voix!

Oh! Une voix pas encore posée comme il faut. Pas tout à fait à sa juste place. Encore un peu trop de tête . . . au timbre inégal . . . trop haut . . . trop bas . . . par endroits. Mais enfin une voix, nette, claire . . . d'une articulation fluide. Sans bégayer . . . Anne a parlé! Elle parle. Elle lit:

Par taquinerie, le soleil
Traîne son pinceau
Sur les jupes de l'eau
De Madame la Pluie:
Regarde l'arc-en-ciel!

Anne a parlé.

Un miracle? Pourquoi non? Il a bien lieu sur l'autel tous les jours au cours de la messe, n'est-ce pas, le miracle? Le miracle de l'eucharistie qui renouvelle la cène entre chrétiens à la table sainte? Le miracle de la présence, du retour du Christ. Il promet. Il annonce. Il accorde sa visite, sa présence.

Alors pourquoi pas, pour une fois, ce retour ici ou là, parmi nous, entre nous, se demande la vieille dame? Oui ou non as-tu communié il y a une heure au corps et au sang du Christ vivant? Du Christ présent sous les espèces du pain et du vin? se dit-elle.

Oui ou non ce jour est-il dimanche, dimanche de Pâques joyeuses? Fête de la Résurrection? Victoire et retour du Christ ressuscité d'entre les morts?

Cela tu le crois? Tu le crois fermement?

Penses-tu plus malaisé de délier la langue à une enfant que de sortir vivant de sa propre sépulture? Crois-tu plus facile de se lever du tombeau, de reprendre tranquillement sa route et de rejoindre ses amis que . . . de sourire à une petite fille? Qu'est-ce qui peut, à ton avis, être interdit à celui qui a vaincu la mort?

A lui qui pour nous enseigner l'amour et nous assurer la Vie a accepté le supplice de la Croix, quel geste généreux, quelle preuve de tendresse peuvent paraître inconcevables? Pourquoi s'en défendrait-il si tel est son bon plaisir en ce matin de fête?

Tremblante, lèvres blanches, mais sourire extasié, la vieille dame se signe. Puis elle prend dans ses bras Anne qui ne semble même pas consciente du prodige immédiat. L'invisible, l'indéniable présence du Ressuscité. Le retour souriant, discret du supplicié, du crucifié. Le brusque, le mystérieux, le triomphant avènement du «règne» parmi nous, l'espace d'un éclair, en la seule faveur d'une enfant d'homme qui n'avait rien d'autre à offrir en holocauste que l'amour des siens.

Easter Story

The Return

THE CROUPIER'S RAKE SCATTERS THEN REASSEMBLES THE CHIPS ON THE green mat—at the whim of chance that does not care a fig about the players' predicament.

And so it was that whimsical fate, unconcerned about minor questions of race and origin, brought and put together two young persons, Caroline and Robert, on the streets of Paris—this melting pot of people.

While she "came up" from her province in the south of France, he had to cross the Atlantic. To meet each other, without a doubt.

To discover each other, love each other, start a family . . . They confidently decided to do this. And rightly so, since here they are leaning over a crib in which the most beautiful baby in the world is smiling.

Perfectly proportioned, with an amber complexion like velvety sapodillas ripened in the sun. The down on the head frothy, black, and curly around the two brown orchids of the ears. Mouth, hands, and feet like delicate and finely worked seashells.

A success Anne was, this fruit of their love. She was already awake, her eyes particularly expressive. These eyes, in fact, were a little disconcerting, because they alternated between being too bright or not bright enough.

A careful, detached observer would notice it after a while. Sometimes the child's gaze is calm and remote, apparently turned inwards. Other times, it lights up and burns with an intense fire. Exceptional. There is something unusual about it. Caroline and Robert, each on their own, study the child's reactions, at first unconsciously, but later discreetly, keeping their impressions to themselves.

They become more and more clearly aware of the fact that the baby seems not to react to noise—not even to the sound of their voices. They do not dare admit it to themselves. They tacitly refuse to admit it.

Days and weeks go by. And the concern and fear that create anguish in the hearts of young parents keep increasing.

They have to face the facts. Besides, the doctor confirms after an examination that the pretty orchids are empty. The child is deaf.

When a second baby, Michèle, comes into the world, a green-eyed doll, as chubby and pretty as her elder sister, the couple welcomes her. But they can no longer deny the embarrassment of Anne's situation, condemned as she is from birth to total silence and to the deaf-mute's cruel isolation.

"Being there with her all the time, giving her constant attention and care round the clock can be tremendously helpful to her," the specialists assure Caroline.

Staying by her daughter's side? Devoting herself to watching out for the flowering of her sensibility, the awakening of her spirit. Making contact and communication with others better for her? The young mother dreamed of dedicating herself to this! But how to do this? How could she give up her monthly salary without destroying the stability in the family's budget? Contemplate adding the cost of the expensive treatment needed for Anne when expenses that were already heavy were increased by the new addition to the family?

Caroline, more worried every day, becomes more and more taciturn. And Robert too retreats into gloomy silence. What saint can he dedicate himself to? How can he increase his income? How can he earn more so that Caroline can give up working in the office and stay with the child? Ah! If he could only make sure that they would have the services of the best specialists! And provide the best informed and most effective care for the girl!

He secretly reproaches himself, accusing himself of incompetence. His conscience tortures him. "They talk about the influence of the mother on the child during pregnancy. They say that the emotional climate of the home is very important, that it practically determines how the nervous system functions," Robert says over and over to himself, asking himself: "Was I the husband that Caroline needed? Was I able to create the kind of environment around my wife that would have been conducive to a perfect gestation—an environment of serenity and joy, essential for her happiness to blossom—the conditions that could guarantee the most chances of success for our child?"

Robert tries to remember the trivial details of their life during this critical period. Were there arguments? Conflicts between him and his wife? He can't remember. Obviously, some minor arguments, but nothing of any consequence! Never any serious fights. Fun quarrels that ended with delightful making up. No . . . no serious disagreements between them.

But, the husband reflects, what about the family circle? There were a lot of things to discuss, misunderstandings to clear up, areas of potential disagreement to defuse. How many inappropriate questions they had to dodge, mistakes to be sorry for, gaffes to apologize for! "Hey, Robert, your mother really drank a lot of coffee!" or "You're a lucky man! If you don't take a shower, it doesn't show!" When they were first married, how many wisecracking, joking remarks they had to endure in meetings in social settings with people who lacked both tact and information!

When they were by themselves, the young couple almost always laughed about that. Today, Robert is worried sick. Caroline, who is in distress, doesn't confide in him anymore. Their words sometimes turn harsh. Silence now falls between them more and more heavily, loaded with bitterness.

"What's on your mind?," Robert asks ten times a day, ending up by responding to some triviality with: "Say it! Admit that you're sorry you tried drinking that disastrous coffee with cream!"

Caroline is shattered and can't believe her ears! That is what Robert's endless reflections are all about? That is what is behind his very obvious lack of self-confidence and the growing doubt that is poisoning him?

And so it was that after Caroline found herself so profoundly tested as a mother, she found herself further wounded as a wife.

In the face of the danger threatening her family, the young woman puts her own sadness on the back burner. She decides to fight. On all fronts. She needs renewed strength and courage.

Face the situation. First, give up the office. Make do with Robert's salary as an engineer. Perform miracles of organizing and saving to keep the home running. Reduce spending immediately. Dismiss the cleaning lady. Give up all outside help. Do the cooking and laundry herself.

Most of all, most of all!, Caroline advises herself, never be far away from Anne. Watch over her! Don't, for anything in the word, be negligent in caring for her. Do not let my zeal cool or my attention lessen. We will need to include Anne in our activities, in all of our conversations, and, as the speech therapist suggests, always talk to her face-to-face, looking at her straight in the eyes.

"She needs to follow lip and tongue movement. She needs to study the position and the role of the palate," he said, specifying that Anne has not only to figure out and understand the muscular mechanism but also to reproduce it.

"Her mouth needs to patiently follow the outlines of sounds. Her eyes have to be sharp enough to make a picture of them, so that she can give form, color, and meaning to words, despite the deficiency in her ears."

And so well does the mother apply herself, following the demanding instructions faithfully, and so much effort does Caroline put into doing everything she can, persevering tirelessly, that finally success comes!

A first word, a sound grating the tightened vocal cords as it comes out, a hoarse but perceptible sound, a name bursts out of the little girl's lips: "Daddy!"

What balm and sweetness to Robert's heart! Immediately, he is flooded with renewed courage and energy. He now participates in the elocution exercises steadfastly and efficiently. He takes care to articulate carefully whenever he talks to Anne. Just as Caroline does, he separates the syllables one by one and fires them like bullets from his painstaking lips.

Anne makes rapid progress. Little by little, she is able to use more and more short one- or two-syllable words.

Since her sense of observation is specially developed, she is quicker than others in capturing the sense of what is being said from facial expressions. Conversations, contacts, and discussions with her become less difficult. They congratulate her by saying that she is growing in "strength and wisdom" like the child Jesus. We could add: in beauty, since she is very pleasant—neat, careful, and smiling. Apart from the sharpness of her piercing eyes, there is nothing to distinguish her from any other happy girl her age.

Up to this point, Caroline was not that eager to get behind the wheel of a car, but now she takes advantage of her time at home, reviews the driving code, enjoys practicing to drive, and gets her driving license in record time.

Soon, it is she who every day from their Hauts de Seine suburb drops off Michèle and picks her up at her school and Robert at the laboratory.

Anne goes with them. On the way back home, she stops with her mother at the market, at the grocer's, or in any store, depending on what is needed at the time. The girl records new words.

Back at home the work sessions start, commenting on "general knowledge" gained during the trip. Neither Anne nor Caroline lets opportunities or time be wasted. They never fail in their efforts. The speech therapist declares that he is satisfied.

One morning he suggests: "We could hide this little button that would hardly be a bother behind her ear. The body of her hair would hide it and you wouldn't be able to see it."

Anne accepts in good spirits having the device fitted with her curls hiding it. She gets used to it very quickly. And Michèle, who is also growing and becoming more beautiful, takes her part in the family's concern: helping Anne and assisting her parents. She spends all of her spare time with her sister. Games, laughs, and all sorts of activities they do together. They also have disagreements and arguments. That is for the greater good of the elder sister, who gets stimulation from them.

Robert and Caroline conduct endless research and finally discover an excellent day school for children with "hearing problems" in the 15th arrondissement. Henceforth, on her morning outings Caroline separates herself from her oldest daughter, from her husband, and from Michèle.

The school setting turns out to be extremely beneficial to Anne. She makes some very nice friends. All the same, she also appreciates even more her little sister's friendship.

When they go on vacation by the sea or in the mountains, the two girls are inseparable. They are on the same sports teams. Anne, who is attentive, diligent, and less scatterbrained, excels at swimming in the summer, and skiing on the slopes in the winter.

When conversations with others prove to be difficult, which is rare, Michèle intervenes and helps her sister discreetly.

Their life, looked at from the outside, is practically normal. At eight years old, Michèle is in second grade. Anne, who soon will be in sixth grade, gets respectable grades in the institution on the rue des Favorites. This spring, the management is organizing a charity sale there. There are lots and lots of booths in which work done almost exclusively by the students is displayed. From pictures drawn and carefully framed by the children to little works of lace, the whole display is a testament to their skill and their hard work.

The boys mostly worked with cardboard, clay, wood, glass, and even metals. The girls were responsible for thousands of very varied creations: embroidery, lace, yarn, and wool, crocheted, knitted, and woven. In addition to painting, tapestry, and spun work, they worked on pliable wicker, glass pearls, modeling clay, and bookbinding.

And the mothers tried to outdo each other in generosity. On the buffet, large trays were set out with piles of cookies, sandwiches, tarts, flat cakes to tempt the food lovers.

The students with the most experience act as masters of the house, welcoming the visitors and going with them, like hosts conscious of their duties.

Anne, more attractive and radiant than ever in a pink organdy dress with flounces, shows people around the house. She is among the women, if you please!

Because she has been accepted to holy communion this year. Here she is leading one of her personal guests through the hallways—an old lady, a friend of the family. An old woman who in a way is her namesake, since a group of her young friends, godsons, and adopted nephews, one of whom is Anne, of course, christened her "Tantana."

The old lady walks through the rooms, her hand in the hand of her elegant and determined guide. The child does not stop in front of the sketches, whose colors adorn the walls, or at the refreshment counter, where the crush of people makes it difficult to be served.

Anne also ignores the magic fishing booth, where two adolescents, fishing rods in their hands, are knocking themselves out trying to hook an inaccessible prize.

The baby clothes section does not seem interesting to her either. Anne goes straight to a room that is deserted during lunchtime: the bookstore. There are three tables arranged in a semicircle, covered with picture books.

With a confident gesture, the child grabs a volume with a red plastic-coated cover lit up by the smiling face of a black child. Above the picture the title of the book is spread out in large letters: *Antillean Nursery Rhymes and Songs.*

Anne stops without moving for a moment with her eyes closed, as if to collect herself. Then, she opens the book, finds a particular page, and, in the most natural way in the world, declares: "The rainbow. I know your poem, Tantana. Listen. Listen a little. I am going to read it to you."

That takes the old lady's breath away. She props herself up against the wall, leaning so as not to collapse, buckle at the knees, or fall to her knees!

She puts her fist in her mouth, holding back a cry that comes to her lips.

Anne spoke . . . Anne is speaking. Without difficulty. Fluently. Anne is expressing herself with her voice, with her mouth, not with her hands anymore. Cheerfully, easily, like you or like me, Anne is making herself heard. She is hearing herself speak! She is controlling her voice!

Oh! A voice not quite as steady as it should be. Not exactly in its right place. Still a little too much from the head, with an uneven tone to it—too low or too high in places. But finally a bright, clear voice, its articulation smooth. Without stuttering . . . Anne spoke! She is speaking. She reads:

The sun, teasing,
Drags his paintbrush
On the water skirts
Of Mrs. Rain
Look at the rainbow!

Anne spoke.

A miracle? Why not? Doesn't a miracle take place every day on the altar during mass? The miracle of the Eucharist that re-creates the Last Supper for Christians at the holy table? The miracle of Christ's presence and of his return? He promises, He announces, He grants his visit, his presence. So why can He not, for once, return here or there, among us, between us, the old lady asks herself? Did you not receive communion an hour ago in the body and blood of the living Christ, yes or no? Of Christ present in the form of bread and wine? she asks herself. Yes or no, is today Sunday, joyous Easter Sunday? Feast of the Resurrection? Victory and return of Christ risen from the dead?

Do you believe that? Do you truly believe it?

Do you think it is more difficult to free the tongue of a child than to come out alive from your own tomb? Do you think it is easier to rise from the grave, to resume your journey quietly and return to your friends than . . . to smile at a little girl? What, in your opinion, can be beyond the reach of him who conquered death?

What act of generosity, what mark of affection can seem to be inconceivable for him, who in order to teach us love and ensure life for us accepted the agony of the cross? Why would he not do it if it pleased him to do so on this holiday morning?

Shaking, her lips white, smiling in ecstasy, the old lady makes the sign of the cross. Then, she takes Anne in her arms, who does not even seem to be conscious of the wonder of the moment. The invisible, undeniable presence of the Risen. The smiling, discreet return of the persecuted, of the crucified. The sudden, mysterious, triumphant advent of the "reign" amongst us, as quick as lightning, only on account of a child of man who had nothing else to offer in sacrifice than the love of his own people.

Conte de Noël

«A chaque cochon son samedi.»

—Proverbe antillais

*Conte dédié à ceux qui savent les finesses de notre langage
créole, en goûtent l'esprit, apprécient la profondeur, la densité
des sentences qui en corsent l'expression.*

S'IL PEUT PARAÎTRE LOGIQUE DE SOULIGNER ICI L'USAGE COURANT DE NOS
proverbes, il est superflu de préciser le sens de celui-ci «A chaque cochon,
son samedi.»

Le samedi n'est-ce pas le jour du boudin? Tandis qu'autour du feu de
bois les uns grattent d'une lame rapide les soies de la couenne ébouillantée,
les autres s'affairent autour du baquet de sang encore chaud. Bouquets de
persil frais, d'oignons odoriférants, piments verts, piments rouges, entassés
auprès du hachoir.

Oui. Pour chaque porc se lève le samedi où, par tradition, s'accomplit
son destin.

Ainsi de chacun de nous. Allusion à notre dernière heure? Pas néces-
sairement. Le proverbe fait mieux. D'une façon plus large, il nous rappelle
les conséquences tout aussi inéluctables de nos actes et de notre comportement.

A chacune de nos initiatives, son aboutissement inévitable. Quelque
part s'inscrit à notre débit le coût de chacune de nos erreurs. Le châtiment
immédiat ou lointain, de chacune de nos fautes . . . de même que . . . Mais
écoutez plutôt.

Il était une fois, en Martinique, un couple de pauvres gens. Pas tout à
fait du modèle courant. Un couple assemblé par le hasard, lié par l'amour,
d'accord. Mais disparate au possible.

La femme? Une de nos paysannes: jambes longues, racées, col droit,
cheveu crépu sous le madras à rayures . . . la joue sombre satinée comme
peau d'aubergine mûre.

Izapu, brun et bouclé, de type méditerranéen, l'homme, lui, venait de loin. En sa ville natale d'un petit État d'Europe Centrale, il avait assisté à l'assassinat de ses parents au cours d'un combat de rues. Autour de sa huitième année.

Poussé par on ne sait quel caprice du sort, il avait atterri un jour en Martinique.

Le cœur à jamais endeuillé, la sensibilité ombrageuse. Il animait d'un souffle amer son pinceau d'artiste peintre. Assez précaire gagne-pain.

Il se peut que s'en souviennent aujourd'hui encore quelques-uns des habitués aux faubourgs de Fort-de-France: ruelles des Terres-Sainville ou du Morne Abella. Les faits ne remontent pas très loin. En tout cas je pourrais nommer celui de mes amis, mécène à ses heures, qui soutint l'artiste de son estime et l'aida de sa bourse.

Fin connaisseur en tableaux, maître X a laissé une riche collection dont plusieurs œuvres signées du nom à consonnance arménienne.

Donc un couple inattendu, mal apparié, mais scellé, authentifié, béni sinon légalisé, par la venue d'un radieux bébé.

L'amour dans l'insécurité, mais l'amour tout de même. Un soir de Noël, plus démunis encore que de coutume, l'homme et la femme se retrouvèrent face à face auprès du berceau. Désespéré, le fusain au bout des doigts, le peintre entreprit de faire un croquis de l'enfant en sommeil.

A défaut d'un bijou à la femme, d'un jouet à enfant, il offrirait au moins ce pieux cadeau à la mère.

Au bout de la seconde des trois messes de Noël, celle dite de «l'aurore» l'étude était achevée. Un chef-d'œuvre avait jailli du pinceau.

Pour la première fois, inspiré de sa seule ferveur, affranchi de toute angoisse, le peintre avait réussi au-delà de toute espérance.

La tête inclinée sur l'oreiller, les paupières closes, lourdes de sommeil, la moue des lèvres humides de lait, expression, incarnation d'innocence, d'abandon, de foi tranquille, totale en la vie, l'enfant reposait.

Conscient de la perfection de sa réalisation, l'homme tout fier en fit don à la femme. Elle estima le cadeau à sa double valeur, artistique et sentimentale.

Désormais, son bien le plus précieux après l'enfant. L'année qui suivit leur fut hélas! cruelle. La misère s'accrut. Le mauvais sort s'acharnait.

L'artiste se mit à boire, et l'enfant, nerveux, à se porter mal.

La femme ne savait plus à quel saint se vouer. Le jour où, de guerre lasse, ils décidèrent de se séparer, ils crurent, l'un et l'autre, adopter la solution la meilleure.

Comment emporter chacun la moitié de leur seul avoir commun, l'enfant? D'ailleurs quel soin le père pourrait-il en prendre, tout seul? En vraie mère antillaise, la femme s'en chargerait. Elle s'effaçait de la vie de l'homme mais elle gardait son enfant.

Résigné, l'homme renonçait à l'une et à l'autre. En retour, il suppliait que lui soit rendu le fusain de Noël, le portrait de l'enfant endormi.

Un instant, la femme, douloureuse, songea au refus. Le tableau lui appartenait en propre.

Les yeux brouillés de larmes, ils fixaient tous les deux, avec une ardeur égale, un égal désespoir, la toile accrochée au mur.

A la même seconde, un cri leur déchira les entrailles. Illusion? Miracle? Le visage de l'enfant s'animait, s'était animé, là, devant eux.

Un sourire où perlait une goutte de lait, creusait des fossettes aux joues . . . Entre les paupières levées s'offrait le regard lumineux, rayonnant de tendresse, de confiance.

Le couple se retrouva à genoux, comme devant la crèche de Noël. Bouleversés, éperdus, l'homme et la femme s'étreignirent.

Ils surent que désormais plus rien au monde ne les séparerait. Aucune détresse plus jamais ne viendrait à bout de leur courage, n'entamerait leur amour, ne menacerait leur foi en la joie permanente, quotidienne de Noël.

A chaque cochon son samedi . . . chaque jour son crépuscule . . . chaque vie son déclin, ai-je dit?

Ne suffit-il pas de changer l'ordre des mots pour buter sur d'autres évidences, éclatantes, lumineuses, triomphantes, elles?

Puisqu'aussi bien l'aube vient au bout de toute nuit . . . puisque la vie surgit de la mort elle-même . . . pourquoi ne pas proclamer à leur tour ces vérités:

A chaque samedi sa corne d'abondance, chaque samedi son cortège de promesses, chaque samedi sa moisson de joie, chaque amour son apothéose!

Christmas Story

"Every Pig Has His Saturday"
—Caribbean proverb

*This story is dedicated to those who know the subtleties of our
Creole language, who enjoy its wit and appreciate the depth
and the density of the maxims that spice up its expression.*

IF IT MAY SEEM LOGICAL TO STRESS HERE THAT OUR PROVERBS ARE COM-
monly used, there is no need to specify the meaning of this one: "Every pig
has his Saturday."

Isn't Saturday pudding day? Around the wood fire some folks are scrap-
ing off the bristles from the boiled skin of the pig with their quick blades,
while others are bustling around the tub of still warm blood. Bunches of
fresh parsley, fragrant onions, green peppers, and red peppers are stacked
around the chopping board.

Yes. For each pig gets up on Saturday, when by tradition his destiny is
accomplished. And it is like that for every one of us. Is this a reference to
our final hour? Not necessarily. The proverb does better than that. In a larger
context, it reminds us of the similarly inevitable consequences of our actions
and our behavior.

Each of our initiatives bears its inevitable outcome. The cost of each
one of our errors is inscribed somewhere on our account—the punishment,
either immediate or far away, for each of our mistakes . . . just as . . . But
listen instead.

Once upon a time, in Martinique, there were a couple of good poor
people. Not exactly like those you see today. A couple brought together by
coincidence, linked by love, yes, but as badly matched as you could imagine.

The wife? She was one of our countrywomen with long legs like a thor-
oughbred, a straight neck, frizzy hair under a striped madras, cheeks dark
and satin-smooth like the skin of a ripe eggplant.

Izapu, the husband, dark and curly-haired, a Mediterranean type, was from far away. In his native town, in a little Central European state, he had witnessed his parents' murder during a street fight when he was about eight.

He had landed one day in Martinique, as a result of some mysterious whim of fate. With a heart left forever in mourning, and a touchy sensitivity, he wielded his artist's paintbrush with a tinge of bitterness. Painting, a rather precarious profession.

Possibly some of the people who used to frequent the suburbs of Fort-de-France—the narrow streets of Terres-Sainville or Morne Abella—might still remember them. It wasn't that long ago that these events occurred. I can even give you the name of one of my friends, a patron of the arts when the fancy took him, who supported the artist with respect and also helped him financially.

A connoisseur of paintings, Master X has left a rich collection, several of which were signed with an Armenian-sounding name.

This unexpected, mismatched couple, therefore, was sealed, blessed, and even legalized, by the arrival of a beaming baby.

Love in insecurity, but still love. One Christmas night, the man and woman, more destitute than usual, found themselves facing each other over the crib. The painter, in despair, with his charcoal pencil in hand, started making a sketch of the sleeping child.

Unable to provide jewelry for his wife or a toy for his child, he would at least offer this pious gift to the mother.

By the end of the second of the three Christmas masses, the one called "dawn," his drawing was finished. A masterpiece had sprung forth from the brush.

For the first time, inspired only by his enthusiasm, freed of all anguish, the painter had succeeded beyond all expectation.

Head tilted on the pillow, eyelids closed, heavy with sleep, a mouth pouting and damp with milk, the expression the incarnation of innocence, relaxation, and tranquil and complete faith in life, the child rested.

Conscious of the perfection of his achievement, the man proudly gave it to his wife. She appreciated the gift for its double value, artistic and sentimental.

From that time on, this was her most precious possession after the child. Alas, the year that followed was cruel. Their poverty and destitution increased. Bad luck hounded them. The artist started drinking and the child became nervous and its health turned bad.

The woman did not know what saint to appeal to. The day came when out of desperation they decided to separate, both thinking they were adopting the best solution.

But how could they each take half of the only thing they had in common, the child? Besides, what care could the father provide on his own? As a true Antillean mother, the woman would take care of the child. She was withdrawing from the man's life, but she was keeping her child.

The man, resigned, gave them both up. In return, he begged that the Christmas charcoal drawing be given back to him, the portrait of the child sleeping. For a moment, the wife in distress thought about refusing; the portrait was really hers.

Eyes misted with tears, they stared with equal ardor and desperation at the canvas up on the wall. At that same second, a scream curdled their insides. Was it an illusion? A miracle? The face of the child lit up, had become animated, right there in front of them.

A smile, with a drop of milk standing out, formed dimples in the child's cheeks. And between the open eyelids was a luminous look, beaming with tenderness and confidence.

The couple found themselves kneeling, as if they were in front of the nativity scene. Overwhelmed and overcome with emotion, the man and woman embraced each other.

They knew that henceforth nothing in the world would ever come between them. Never again would any crisis deplete their courage, damage their love, or threaten their faith in the permanent and daily joy of Christmas.

Did I say that every pig has its Saturday . . . every day its dusk . . . every life its end?

Wouldn't just changing the order of words be enough for us to stumble on other truths—dazzling, luminous, and triumphant?

Since dawn comes at the end of every night, since life comes from death itself, why not proclaim these truths:

Each Saturday has its horn of plenty, each Saturday its procession of promises, each Saturday its harvest of joy, and every love its apotheosis!

Le Cadeau

—Fais voir un peu ces cartons, tu veux, ma tante? «Union française universitaire. Cercle culturel international. Comité d'Action du Spectacle. Club de Théâtre des Nations . . . Et puis encore . . . et encore. Sans compter les Associations des Gens d'Outremer! Tu as appartenu, tu appartiens à tous ces groupements? A cette kyrielle de syndicats . . . de Mouvements pour . . . ceci . . . contre cela?

—Pourquoi pas? C'est preuve de quoi, selon toi?

—Probablement de sens social, d'esprit de solidarité. J'ajouterais . . . d'un certain instinct grégaire . . . Sans nuance péjorative aucune!

—Oh! J'en ai entendu d'autres tu sais! Après en avoir considéré le nombre, une collègue, un rien rosse, a eu ce commentaire: Voilà qui vous pose ma chère!

—Elle ironisait!

—Je conviens qu'elle avait raison. Tous ces cartons me classent en effet de manière irréfutable—et bouffonne—parmi les poires de notre société.

—Parce que? Ces pièces seraient preuves de naïveté sinon de vanité?

—En voici une datée de 1936, une de 1938 . . . la dernière, de 1979. Ça fait, échelonné sur quarante années et davantage, un total de 20, 30, cinquante participations.

—Toute une vie!

—Autant d'associations, autant de cotisations consenties donc autant de mérites au titre de gogo, tu ne crois pas?

—Ça dépend desquels. Il y a le choix.

—En effet. S'il fallait recommencer, il n'est pas dit que je me récuserais à chaque fois. Vois ces trois là par exemple, ils me causent de la fierté!

—Comme membre de la S.P.A. Tu veux dire?

—Société protectrice des animaux, N° 109237. Parfaitement! Et puis, ici, «les Amis des bêtes» carton rose, 1957, membre fondateur. Carton blanc, membre à vie, 1960. Président, Dr. F. Méry. Célèbre pour son amour des animaux.

—Est-ce que tu serais pessimiste, ma tante? Façon de dire, avec tes cartons «Plus je connais les hommes, plus j'aime mon chien?»

—Pas du tout! Ils me rappellent nombre de souvenirs, ces vieux cartons. C'est simple!

—De bons souvenirs?

—Ils me font revivre, figure-toi une histoire dont les fées ne sont peut être pas tout à fait exclues. Une sorte de conte de Noël . . . avec miracle à la clé s'il te plaît.

—Des petits miracles de rien du tout. Pas un vrai, grand miracle de Noël?

—Evidemment pas. Enfin, juge toi-même.

C'était en 1957. Je traînais une difficile convalescence dans Paris. Un pathelin [*sic*] à fuir par quiconque n'est pas au maximum de sa forme physique et morale . . . J'avais un de ces cafards! Amis et connaissances ne me manquaient pas, mais je n'avais aucun désir de revoir qui que ce soit après une très longue absence.

Un jour que je me trouvais presque sans l'avoir décidé au sixième étage d'un grand magasin, je suivis la file de gens intéressés par une exposition d'animaux. Les «Amis des Bêtes» présentaient des chiens à adopter.

Les plantes, les bêtes, tout ce qui est vivant m'émeut. Une fois, j'ai eu tout le mal du monde à me débarrasser d'un chat qui s'était mis à me suivre par hasard dans une rue, au cours de vacances dans un village de Normandie.

Les animaux me flairent. Me reconnaissent pour un des leurs. J'en suis toujours très touchée. Je rentrai donc du magasin parisien avec un nouvel ami, un chien, et un des trois cartons en question.

Pourquoi ce menu loulou à longs poils mal peignés plutôt qu'un autre? Ni jeune, ni fringant, ni plus tout à fait blanc. Sa robe déjà prenait nuance coquille d'œuf assez accusée.

Justement peut-être pour toutes ces raisons, il ne faisait envie à personne. Je l'emportai. Sans réfléchir le moins du monde aux conséquences de cette adoption.

Que faire d'un animal alors qu'on se trouve soi-même moralement à la charge d'autrui?

Aussi embarrassés l'un que l'autre nous nous reconnaissions l'un et l'autre pour perdus, le loulou et moi.

Méfiant, il n'abusait ni de familiarité ni de nourriture. Par crainte d'être maltraité probablement, il se détournait obstinément de la porte de la cuisine. Il avait dû y subir maints châtiments dans le passé. Même pour prendre son repas il refusait d'y entrer. Il fallait en sortir son écuelle et la lui proposer ailleurs.

Au bout de quelques semaines je reprenais avec soulagement le bateau vers mes Antilles. Mon chien ne s'en plaignit point.

Tous les jours au cours de la traversée j'allai lui rendre visite au chenil. Nous faisions quelques tours sur le pont promenade. Il y prenait plaisir.

A notre arrivée, le chien semblait découvrir la terre et le climat qui lui convenaient. Complètement transformé, épanoui, heureux, c'était un nouvel hôte. Je me mis à l'appeler Joy. Désormais il méritait ce nom.

Il courait au soleil, aboyait à tous les échos. Il nous accablait tous d'attentions. Dévorait la nourriture exotique, même légumes et fruits: ananas, pain-bois, igname, canne à sucre . . . Nous habitions la maison basse du plateau Didier que tu connais.

—«La maison aux mille persiennes»?

—Avec le grand jardin et les beaux arbres, oui. Joy rajeunissait à vue d'œil tant il s'y plaisait.

—Tu dis qu'il paraissait vieux?

—Aucun doute possible. Joy avait un long passé. Une longue vie de chien derrière lui. Laquelle? Pas rose tous les jours, selon toute vraisemblance. Les souvenirs douloureux l'avaient trop longtemps poursuivi.

De ses expériences nous ignorions tout. Nous ignorions aussi et surtout qu'il saisissait nos propos. Et qui sait? devinait parfois nos intentions.

—Et quoi encore?

—Tu vas voir. Lors de notre première rencontre, au moment de lui passer son collier tout neuf je lui avais remarqué un kyste. Vers l'épaule, dans l'épaisseur du pelage.

Les misères, les ans nous laissent tares et cicatrices. J'en savais personnellement un bon bout sur la question. Acceptées, classées, celles de Joy ne me préoccupaient guère.

Il fallut pourtant les prendre au sérieux après certaine visite au vétérinaire. Il me dit mon chien sérieusement touché.

—«Mais docteur il tient encore bon! Il est heureux.»

—«Si vous voulez. Mais pas pour longtemps. Il va falloir vous résoudre à le faire piquer d'ici peu. Ça vaudra mieux croyez-moi!»

A la maison désormais Joy était l'objet de mille soins. De ceux qui empoisonnent les jours des condamnés.

Attendris, angoissés nous suivions ses ébats. Heureux de le regarder faire. Etonnés, ravis du moindre de ses élans, de la moindre manifestation d'activité. Tout en étant prêts à le calmer. Comme pour l'amener à économiser son énergie. Pour le forcer à durer.

Un jour le vétérinaire consulté par téléphone nous convainquit de ne plus temporiser. Il nous proposait de passer chez nous dans la soirée pour un dernier avis. Après quoi on prendrait un rendez-vous décisif.

Ce jour-là Joy ne se montra d'humeur ni plus abattue ni plus chagrine que d'ordinaire. Il continua à faire celui qui joue les bien-portants pour rassurer son entourage.

A notre profonde stupéfaction le vétérinaire ne le trouva pas à la maison. Sourd à l'appel de nos voix il devait, selon nous, se cacher dans le garage ou le jardin. On explora coins et recoins. En pure perte.

Pas de Joy. Évanoui. Disparu.

Avant de fermer les portes, au coucher, on lui déposa une écuelle garnie sous la véranda. Ainsi il se nourrirait en rentrant au cours de la nuit.

—Il est rentré sans faire de bruit?

—Il n'a jamais reparu. Aujourd'hui encore, le cœur serré, je confesse que personne n'y a rien compris.

—Vous l'avez fait chercher?

—Tu penses! Démarches, enquêtes, recherches sont demeurés vaines. Joy n'est jamais revenu. Nul ne l'a rencontré, n'a buté sur lui mort ou vif.

C'était l'avant-veille de Noël, sa disparition. Les courses, les soucis, les occupations de la dernière semaine de décembre nous absorbant beaucoup, nous ne parlions que peu de notre peine.

Nous espérions d'ailleurs le retour de Joy. Une certaine expérience, vieille de plusieurs années autorisait, réconfortait notre attente.

—L'aventure du chat Mangot?

—Justement! La fois où chien et chat nous avaient suivis en vacances à la mer . . . Apparemment adversaires, mais apparemment seulement, Max, notre cocker irlandais et Mangot—un matou jaunâtre, se chamaillaient à longueur de journée.

Les vacances écoulées, au moment de rentrer à la maison bagages embarqués, panier d'osier ouvert, on cherche le Mangot pour l'inviter à prendre place.

De deux heures nous avons dû retarder le départ! Deux heures passées à l'appeler, l'amadouer, l'aguicher de la voix! Deux heures à explorer les broussailles. Pas plus de chat aux alentours que de pigeon dans mon chapeau!

De guerre lasse nous prenons enfin la route, secrètement persuadés d'avoir été bernés par quelque sacripant du bord de mer. Il y en a qui, pour varier le poisson du menu, se font, avec des haricots rouges et du lapin approximatif, gratuit, un cassoulet nouvelle manière.

Nous n'osions nous l'avouer, mais nous avions renoncé à revoir jamais notre Mangot. C'était jugement erroné! Huit jours après, arrivant on ne sait d'où, Mangot regagnait la maison. En pleine nuit!

Chargé de nous l'annoncer, Max nous sortait du sommeil. Par jappements bruyants, obstinés, joyeux, il nous invitait à ouvrir, à courir au devant du «chat prodigue» rentrant au bercail.

Forts de ce souvenir, longtemps, nous attendîmes Joy. Il n'est pas revenu . . .

A moins que, croyant au miracle, il ne te vienne certain doute. Comme à moi. Quand tu sauras cette autre histoire, toute aussi vraie, je te le jure, qui vient en conclusion. Crois ce que bon te semble, mais ne doute pas de ma parole.

L'année d'après, au Noël suivant le mystérieux départ de Joy, j'y pensais avec quelque mélancolie.

Et voici ce qui arriva. Je partis pour la ville . . .

—Tu passais toujours à la campagne ton temps libre?

—Oui mais je me proposais d'assister à la messe de minuit en la

Cathédrale de Fort-de-France. Nous devions nous réunir ensuite pour un réveillon plutôt calme. Tout juste, histoire d'être en compagnie.

Après la cérémonie, un jeune chien nous emboîta le pas sur le chemin du retour. Sautillant autour de nous, il nous faisait fête. Comme il se frottait à mes chevilles je m'arrêtai, lui caressant le crâne de la main.

«Tu es gentil. Et ton intérêt me flatte . . . Mais va-t-en retrouver ton maître! Rentre chez toi!»

C'était un chiot de belle race. Un chien-loup à ce qu'on pouvait supposer. Haut sur pattes, le poil brun, il dressait de longues belles oreilles.

Il ne fallait absolument pas que se détournant de ses maîtres—probablement tout à côté, il se perdît dans les rues. Je le chassai vertement.

Mais plus je l'éloignais et plus il s'attachait à me suivre. A la maison nous dûmes l'héberger. J'étais tranquille.

Dans cette ville grande comme la main, les animaux de ce prix ne pululent [*sic*] pas me disais-je. Un chien de race, une bête de luxe! On aura vite fait de retrouver ses maîtres. De plus, il n'y a en tout et pour tout que deux vétérinaires dans le pays, tous les deux, des amis. Il sera facile de savoir qui, de leur clientèle, possède famille de chiens loups. La chose est plutôt rare dans notre île.

Au matin du 25 décembre je téléphonai à qui de droit. Je me déclarai détentrice malgré moi d'une bête qui me semblait de valeur et sans doute était recherchée.

Ni le commissariat de police alerté sur le champ, ni le service vétérinaire, ensuite les petites annonces, rien ni personne jamais ne révéla l'origine du chiot.

Le vétérinaire le déclara âgé de six mois. De race parfaitement pure. Je le fis visiter, vacciner, soigner en attendant la venue de ceux qui le réclameraient.

Il ne vint jamais personne.

Quatorze ans, nous avons lui et moi, partagé le pain, le sel de l'amitié. Je le nommai Joy lui aussi.

Joie. Don de Noël. Mais que ne pouvons-nous, avec un peu de foi, attendre de ce jour béni entre les jours?

The Gift

"Can I see these boxes, Auntie?—French University Union. International Cultural Group. Theater Action Committee. Nations Theater Club . . . And so on . . . and so forth. Not to mention the Association of Overseas People. You used to belong, you still belong, to all of these groups? To this host of unions . . . of movements for this, against that?"

"Why not? What does that mean, in your opinion?"

"Probably a social sense, a spirit of solidarity. I would add . . . a certain gregarious instinct . . . And not in any pejorative sense!"

"Oh! I've heard a lot of other things, you know! One of my women colleagues, after reflecting on how many there were, made this comment: 'That really puts you up there, my dear!'"

"She was being ironic!"

"I admit she was right. All these boxes really classify me irrefutably and farcically amongst the suckers of society."

"Because? So these pieces would indicate naiveté, if not vanity?"

"Here's one dated 1936, one from 1938 . . . the last one, from 1979. Spread over forty years and more, that makes a total of twenty, thirty, fifty memberships."

"A whole life!"

"So many organizations, so many subscriptions paid, and therefore so many qualifications for the big-shot title, don't you think?

"It depends which ones. There is a choice."

"Evidently. If I had to do it all over again, I wouldn't necessarily decline in every case. Take these three, for example; they make me feel proud!"

"Like being a member of the S.P.A., you mean?"

"Society for the Protection of Animals, N° 109237. Exactly! And then here, "Friends of Animals," in the pink box, 1957, founding member. White box, life member, 1960. President, Dr. F. Méry. Famous for his love of animals."

"Are you being a pessimist, Auntie? As if you're saying with your boxes, 'The more people I know, the more I love my dog?'"

"Not at all! These old boxes bring back a lot of memories. That's all!"

"Good memories?"

"They actually make me relive a story from which fairies are perhaps not completely excluded. A kind of Christmas story . . . with a miracle at the end of it all, if you please."

"Little insignificant miracles. Not a real, big Christmas miracle?"

"Of course not. Well, judge for yourself."

"It was in 1957. I was having a difficult time convalescing in Paris. The last town to be in for someone who is not in their maximum physical and moral shape . . . I was feeling so low! Not that I didn't have friends and acquaintances, but I had no desire to see anyone after having been away for such a long time.

"One day, finding myself on the sixth floor of a department store, almost without intending to be there, I followed a line of people attracted by a display of animals. The "Friends of Animals" were displaying dogs for adoption.

"Plants, animals, all living things move me. Once, I had a terribly hard time getting rid of a cat that started following me by chance on a street while I was on vacation in a village in Normandy.

"Animals smell me. They recognize me as one of them. I am always very touched by this. So I came home from the Parisian store with a new friend, a dog, and one of the three boxes we were talking about.

"Why this tiny dog with long scruffy hair and not another? Not young, or frisky, or completely white anymore. His coat was already beginning to take on the shade rather markedly of an eggshell.

"Precisely maybe for all of these reasons, no one wanted him. I took him. Without at all thinking about the consequences of this adoption.

"What to do with an animal when we ourselves are morally dependent on others?

"Loulou and I were both equally embarrassed and we both recognized ourselves as lost. He was wary of being too familiar or eating too much food. Probably out of fear of being mistreated, he stubbornly turned away from the kitchen door. That must have been where he was subjected to many punishments in the past. Even to have his meal, he refused to enter the kitchen. His bowl needed to be taken out and offered to him somewhere else.

"At the end of a few weeks, it was a relief to take the ship back to my Caribbean. My dog didn't complain at all.

"Every day during the crossing I went to visit him in the kennel. We took a few strolls on the deck. He enjoyed doing that.

"When we arrived, the dog seemed to discover a land and climate that suited him. Completely transformed, radiant, and happy, he was a new dog. I started calling him Joy. From that time, he deserved that name.

"He ran in the sun, barked at every echo. He showered us all with attention. He devoured the exotic food, even vegetables and fruit: pineapples, breadfruit, yams, sugar cane . . . We lived in the low-roofed house on the Didier plateau that you know."

"The house with the thousand shutters?"

"Yes. With the large garden and the beautiful trees. Joy loved it so much he grew younger before our very eyes."

"Are you saying that he seemed old?"

"Without any possible doubt. Joy had a long past. A long dog life behind him. What kind of life? Not a bed of roses every day, in all likelihood. Painful memories had followed him for too long.

"We knew nothing about his experiences. We also and above all did not know that he understood what we were saying, and, who knows, sometimes perhaps guessed our intentions."

"So what happened?"

"You'll see. When I first met him, and as I went to put on his brand new collar, I had noticed he had a cyst. In the thick fur near his shoulder.

"Woes and years leave us with flaws and scars. I personally knew quite a lot about that matter. I'd accepted and filed away Joy's flaws and scars, so I hardly thought about them.

"However, after a certain visit to the veterinarian, I had to take them seriously. He told me my dog had a serious condition.

"But, doctor, he is still holding up well! He is happy."

"Maybe. But not for long. We will need to decide to put him to sleep soon. That will be better, believe me!"

"From that time on, Joy was shown a host of attentions at home, the kind that make the days of condemned people a living hell. We were emotional and worried, and followed his frolics, happy to see him do his thing. We were surprised and delighted at the slightest liveliness that he showed, of the slightest sign of activity on his part, ready all the while to calm him down, as if to get him to save his energy, to force him to hold on.

"One day, the vet whom we had consulted by phone convinced us not to delay any longer. He offered to come by in the evening for a last opinion after which we would make a final appointment.

"That day, Joy's mood was no more dejected or sad than usual. He continued to put on a show of good health to reassure everyone around him.

"To our profound astonishment, the vet did not find him at home. We thought that he was ignoring our voices calling for him and had to be hiding in the garage or the garden. We explored every nook and cranny. No luck.

"No Joy. Vanished. Disappeared.

"At bedtime, before we closed the doors we put out a full bowl for him under the veranda, so that he would eat when he came back home during the night."

"Did he come back home without making any noise?"

"He never resurfaced. Still to this day, with pain in my heart, I confess that no one understood anything about this."

"You had people searching for him?"

"Of course! Nothing came of the inquiries, investigations, and searches. Joy never came back. No one came across him or stumbled upon him dead or alive."

"The day of his disappearance was the day before Christmas Eve. Since we were very much involved in the shopping and the concerns and activities of the last week of December, we hardly talked at all about our trouble.

"Besides, we were hoping that Joy would return. A certain experience, from a few years before, gave us reason and comfort to wait."

"The adventure of Mangot the cat?"

"Exactly! The time when dog and cat followed us on vacation to the sea . . . Max, our Irish spaniel, and Mangot, a yellowish tomcat, seemingly enemies, but only seemingly, squabbled all day long.

"At the end of the vacation, as we were getting ready to go home, luggage loaded and wicker basket open, we're looking for Mangot to invite him to take his place. Two hours we had to push back our departure! Two hours spent calling him, coaxing him, enticing him with our voices! Two hours searching in the bushes. No more cats around than pigeons in my hat!

"We finally give up and get on the road, secretly convinced we were the victims of some seashore rascal. Some of them, for a change from fish on the menu, make themselves a new type of casserole, with red beans and a kind of free rabbit.

"We didn't dare admit it to ourselves, but we had given up on ever seeing our Mangot again. Our judgment was incorrect! Eight days later, coming from who knows where, Mangot reaches home again. In the middle of the night!

"Max, who had the task of giving us the news, woke us from our sleep. With loud, stubborn, happy yelps, he invited us to open the door, and greet the 'prodigal cat' returning to the fold.

"Strengthened by this memory, we waited for Joy for a long time. He didn't come back . . .

"Unless, if you believe in miracles, you have some doubt—as I do—when you hear this other story that I'm going to end with, which is also just as true, I swear. Believe whatever you like, but don't doubt my words.

"The following year, at the Christmas after Joy's mysterious departure, I was thinking about it with some melancholy.

"And this is what happened. I left to go into town . . ."

"You always spent your spare time in the countryside?"

"Yes, but I was planning to attend midnight mass at the Fort-de-France cathedral. We were supposed to get together afterwards for a fairly quiet Christmas Eve supper. Just to be in one another's company.

"After the ceremony, as we were making our way back home, a young dog started following close behind us. He skipped and jumped around us, fawning on us. As he was rubbing against my ankles, I stopped, petting his head with my hand.

"'You are nice. And I'm flattered by your interest. But scat! Go find your master! Go back home!'

"It was a nice breed of puppy. An Alsatian, one would assume. Tall on his paws, with brown hair, and long, beautiful ears held high.

"On no account could he be allowed to wander away from his master, who was probably nearby, and get lost in the streets. I chased him away sharply.

"But the more I chased him, the more he insisted on following me. We had to put him up at home. I was at peace.

"In this town that was no bigger than a hand, animals as expensive as this are not found just anywhere, I told myself. A real purebred, a luxury animal! It won't take long to find his masters. On top of that, there are only two veterinarians in the country, both of them my friends. It will be easy to find out which one of their clients owns a family of Alsatian dogs. These are rather rare on our island.

"The morning of December 25th, I telephoned all around to find out. I said that I found myself in possession of an animal that seemed to be valuable and was without a doubt being looked for.

"Neither the police station that was immediately informed, nor the veterinary service, nor the small ads, nothing or no one ever revealed the origin of this puppy.

"The veterinarian pronounced him to be six months old. A perfect purebred. I had him examined, vaccinated, and taken care of, as I waited for the people who would claim him to turn up.

"No one ever came.

"For fourteen years, he and I have shared the bread and salt of friendship. Him too I called Joy. Joy. A Christmas present. But, with a little faith, what can we not expect from this most blessed of days?"

Le Capitaine Se Marie

Lèvres pincées, paupières brûlées de veilles, Cendrine tire l'aiguille avec application. Une guirlande de fleurs d'oranger part du col de la robe, s'attarde en bouquets à la ceinture, et court en volutes jusqu'au bas de la jupe.

Riche broderie sur un beau tissu. L'ouvrière n'a regardé ni à la peine, ni à la dépense. Voilà bientôt quinze ans qu'elle amasse des sous pour sa toilette de mariée et que son modèle est choisi.

Au coup de l'angélus du soir, elle pique les derniers points. Son épaule est douloureuse, ses tempes bourdonnent. Mais elle se signe avec joie. Elle a terminé son ouvrage.

Auprès de la croisée, elle installe une chaise-longue et s'étend quelques instants.

Dehors, un reste du jour traîne sur les panaches des cocotiers qui bruissent sur la plage. Les sables brunissent. Les «îlets» mordorés se nuancent de violet.

Dans le ciel persistent des ors et des pourpres à la place où le soleil a disparu. De loin, sur la mer, dont l'indigo se noie peu à peu dans la nuit, Cendrine regarde accourir vers la côte une longue frange d'écume blanche.

Une voisine s'accoude familièrement à la fenêtre.

—Eh bien, Cendrine, il approche le grand jour!

—Plus qu'une semaine, en effet!

—Tant mieux, ma fille, tu as bien assez patienté.

Depuis quinze ans, elle attend.

Brisefer voyage à travers les Antilles. Aux escales, de loin en loin, il griffonne quelques lignes. Tous les deux, trois ans, il arrive à l'improviste.

Pendant une semaine, heureuse, comblée, Cendrine jouit de la chère présence. Parmi d'extraordinaires histoires de marins la voix chaude égrène des mots d'une âpre tendresse.

Puis, la mer lui reprend son fiancé. De nouveau seule dans sa case, à l'ombre des cocotiers, Cendrine prend soin de ses couvées de canetons.

Parfois une femme pousse la porte. Elle dénoue un madras. Des coupes de nansouk s'étalent sur la table. Les enfants manquent de chemises.

Cendrine tourne et retourne le tissu entre ses mains. D'un œil avisé, elle en étudie le rendement.

La cliente est une vieille connaissance. Fille du même «quartier», ancienne compagne de catéchisme ou de jeux, aujourd'hui mère de famille. Volubile, elle vante sa nichée.

—Paulo, tu sais, trotte déjà comme un lapin. Il sait le nom de tous ses frères. A quinze mois!

Cendrine sourit, rêveuse.

—Et toi, chère? Raconte. Quelles nouvelles du capitaine?

Un peu d'ombre aux pommettes, la jeune femme ouvre la cassette aux reliques. Quelques babioles! Un éventail de nacre, de la menue vannerie, des mouchoirs de dentelle vieillie . . . Une poignée de lettres et de cartes postales, timbrées de tous les ports de la Caraïbe et d'ailleurs. Surinam . . . Port-of-Spain . . . Maracaïbo, etc.

Maintenant, tout cela, le passé!

Brisefer est de retour, pour de bon. Dans un instant il viendra, s'installera dans ce fauteuil, tout près d'elle, lui fera sa cour d'homme de mer, à la fois timide et brusque, empressée, silencieuse, tendre et bourrue.

Cendrine ne sent plus la fatigue. Elle tresse ses lourdes nattes, les enroule, y fixe de larges et solides épingles d'écaille. Les mains parfumées d'un brin de vétiver, un soupçon de poudre aux joues, elle se pare d'une longue «gole» blanche ruchée de dentelle au col et aux poignets.

Elle fait un bout de toilette rapide à la pièce. Les bouts de fil et de tissu disparaissent. L'ordre des chaises soigneusement rectifié, l'amoureuse s'assied, l'oreille au guet.

Quelle chance que la *Bonne-Mère* ait été désarmée! Elle vient d'être condamnée, reléguée au cimetière des rafiots. A ce que rapporte Brisefer, sa carrière ne pouvait se prolonger. Elle faisait eau de plus en plus, donnant «une bande» énorme.

Tant pis pour le capitaine, et tant mieux pour la fiancée, puisqu'il a regagné son village et qu'enfin la date du mariage est arrêtée.

Dimanche, à la messe paroissiale, troisième et dernière publication. Sur la plage, le patron de la pirogue *Rénette*, un vieux camarade, interpelle Brisefer.

—Alors, capitaine, l'ancre est jetée?

A califourchon sur la quille d'une barque renversée, Brisefer tend une main distraite. Ses yeux ne quittent pas l'horizon.

Un navire est en vue par bâbord des «bancs de sable». Les deux marins observent, l'œil ardent. Une pipe s'éteint.

—Du feu?

—Vas-y!

Les têtes rapprochées, les brûle-gueules se touchent. Le tabac rougeoie. Enveloppés d'un âcre nuage de fumée, les hommes s'écartent, se retournent vers la mer.

Le brick-goëlette vire de bord. Les focs gonflés, il évolue. Mais le patron de la *Rénette* insiste, taquin.

—Samedi la noce, vieux frère?

—Oui, j'y viens tard, mais j'y viens tout de même.

—Vraiment, plaisante Cirba, marin débarqué vaut cavalier désarçonné. Quand les planches du pont manquent sous les pieds, on n'est plus guère bon qu'à faire des sottises.

Sans accuser le coup, Brisefer s'exclame:

—Superbe brick! Sais-tu de quel port?

—Ma foi, non. L'usine attend des traverses de Norvège, et, de Surinam, un moteur.

Une forte brise déroule la flamme au sommet du grand mât. Les deux hommes la saluent d'un même élan.

Les yeux abrités de la main, ils se penchent dans la direction du navire qui file vers la Caravelle.

Ils longent la côte parallèlement au brick, critiquant la manœuvre.

Mais les roches de la pointe leur barrent le passage. Ils s'en retournent à regret.

Brusquement, Brisefer s'appuie à l'épaule de Cirba:

—Après tout, une bien brave fille, pas vrai?

—Cendrine? Pour ça, oui!

—Alors j'ai raison, camarade! A quarante ans, on doit jeter du lest. Et puis, chacun son tour de prendre femme, d'être «emmignonné» hein, vieux scélérat!

Mais Cirba n'écoute plus. Un coup de sifflet de l'usine le rappelle à son poste.

Les hommes de la *Rénette* préparent un chargement de barils de tafia. Les wagons sont prêts. Les mulets attelés l'un devant l'autre entre les rails, dressent l'oreille, ombrageux.

Un claquement sec de la langue . . . Ils partent à petits pas vers le quai où les pirogues vides se balancent, à fleur d'eau.

Cirba fait le pointage.

Resté seul, Brisefer, une lorgnette en main, dessine des figurines sur le sable. Une, deux, trois têtes d'enfant . . . Est-ce trop tard?

Il blanchit un peu aux tempes mais garde le cheveu dru, l'œil clair, le pied alerte.

Trop tard? Certainement non. Une vie nouvelle s'ouvre devant lui.

La taille soudain redressée, l'allure fringante, il s'achemine, sifflotant, vers la maison où l'attend Cendrine.

Demain les noces. Tantes, grands oncles, cousins et bons amis arrivent des hauteurs environnantes.

Le sacristain taille les arbustes qui longent l'allée conduisant à l'église. A l'intérieur, tout est prêt. Les ors reluisent. Les nappes d'autel sont changées. Des cierges tous neufs se dressent devant la niche où sourit la Vierge Marie.

Au seuil de la mairie le concierge secoue des tapis. Tout le village semble en fête. La femme du vieux Cirba lui lisse avec amour sa meilleure chemise blanche, une «mille plis».

Autour de Cendrine, les commères, importantes, jacassent à qui mieux mieux. La fiancée, affairée, choisit du linge de table, distribue des torchons, sort l'argenterie, les provisions, veille à tout, est partout.

—Cousine Cendrine, montre un peu ta chemise de mariée?

Du linon fin, garni de Valenciennes imitation. Les petites campagnardes admirent, bouche bée.

Fiévreuses, les demoiselles d'honneur cousent des flots de ruban à leurs toilettes bleu-ciel. Elles mettent des fleurs au frais, frisent la dentelle des aumonières.

A la cuisine, grand branlebas. Césarine, une voisine, tord le cou au plus gros des canards. Une autre dépouille un lapin blanc.

Agacé par le va-et-vient de l'assistance, d'heure en heure plus nombreuse, Brisefer, s'est éclipsé. Juché sur une pointe rocheuse au bord d'une crique, il aspire l'air du large lourd de senteurs marines.

Il songe à la *Bonne-Mère*. En carène depuis combien de semaines? Il compte sur ses doigts. Seulement six? Pas possible! Est-ce que des mois et des mois ne sont pas écoulés? Comme le temps dure sur la terre ferme! . . . Une fois marié, il cherchera un nouvel engagement, pour de courtes traversées, bien entendu . . .

A quoi bon se leurrer! Courtes ou longues, ne les fait pas qui veut. Tous les voiliers de quelque importance sont pourvus d'officiers. Aucun poste . . . A moins que quelque vieux loup de mer ne se décide à la retraite.

En attendant, Brisefer, capitaine de la *Bonne-Mère*, goëlette désarmée, taillera dans des noix de coco vidées des petits bateaux pour ses fils. Il rêvera devant la Caraïbe où glisseront des voiliers.

Ces goëlettes, elles hantent son souvenir.

Coquettes, gracieuses, parées comme des filles à marier, ou lasses de bourlinguer, la coque gémissant au vent . . .

La *Marie-Joseph*, son premier commandement . . . *Anabelle*, toute blanche, la voilure haute, la coupe élégante . . . tenant l'eau si vaillamment par n'importe quel temps.

Cette pauvre *Dora-Lise* qui a coulé bas une nuit du côté de Sabbat . . . Un passage infernal . . .

Et jusqu'à la dernière, cette *Bonne-Mère*, si légère à la brise, malgré sa coque défoncée.

Plus belle, plus imposante que toutes, il revoit la *Roxelane*. Un jour il la croisa au large de Cayenne. Mais rapide comme une flèche, elle devança la

Bonne-Mère d'une bonne couple d'heures.

L'ancre jetée, les capitaines se saluèrent au porte-voix et se convièrent mutuellement à la visite de leurs rafiots.

Brisefer s'en souvient, il n'en dormit pas de toute une semaine. Quelle goëlette, mes amis! On n'en trouve plus de cette classe, depuis que ces damnés vapeurs chassent peu à peu les voiliers. Pour un pareil commandement quel capitaine ne donnerait sa part de paradis!

Mais elle est loin la *Roxelane*! Et mortes les ambitions de Brisefer.

Demain, une nouvelle vie . . .

—Enfin, vous voici, Capitaine. Je vous cherche par tout le bourg depuis une heure au moins.

—Que me veux-tu petit?

—Une lettre recommandée à votre adresse. Signez ici.

Surpris, l'homme tourne l'enveloppe entre ses doigts. D'où vient-elle? Peu lui importe! Quelque taquinerie d'un vieux compagnon qui aura appris son mariage. C'est la coutume entre hommes de mer.

Brisefer glisse la lettre dans sa poche, sort sa pipe qu'il allume. Les yeux au loin, il tire de lentes bouffées.

Le temps passe, il faut tout de même rentrer pour déjeuner.

Soudain, ses mains retrouvent l'enveloppe qu'il avait oubliée. Il l'ouvre.

Du papier à en-tête . . . Le nom d'un armateur . . . Les lèvres du vieux marin tremblent . . . Sa vue se brouille.

Dominant son émoi, il lit à haute voix. Est-ce possible, on l'appelle là-bas. On lui propose à lui, Brisefer, le commandement de la *Roxelane*.

Allons donc! C'est une plaisanterie, une farce cruelle imaginée par les copains la veille de son mariage!

Pourtant, cette lettre, officiellement remise par la poste, ce timbre de la Guyane, ce cachet, cette signature . . . sont authentiques.

Le capitaine contient mal une envie de crier sa joie. Se pourrait-il que de nouveau, il soit libre sur la mer, face au soleil, parmi les embruns et le vent? Maître à bord, après Dieu . . . Et à bord . . . de la *Roxelane*!

Qu'attend-il pour se décider, pour se hâter vers le port. Il faut partir, sans tarder. Quelle date, aujourd'hui? Est-ce que le paquebot pour Cayenne ne lève pas l'ancre ce soir même? Oh! Partir, partir! Par n'importe quelle voie gagner Fort-de-France! Arriver à temps . . . Prendre le bateau!

Il dévale la pente, éperdu.

Devant l'usine, une voiture est arrêtée. Des voyageurs en descendent. On décharge des valises.

—Hé! camarade! Retournez-vous en ville?

—Tout de suite, si le cœur vous en dit!

Sans un mot, Brisefer s'installe au fond de la voiture. Elle traverse le bourg, lancée comme un bolide.

Il calcule ses chances d'arriver. Juste le temps! Dire qu'il est à la merci d'une panne stupide!

Vite! Encore plus vite!

Devant ses yeux déjà se déploie la voilure d'une goëlette, étincelante dans la lumière qui baigne la Caraïbe.

Dans l'oubli s'évanouit une robe de soie blanche, finement brodée de fleurs d'oranger, qu'une fois, dans un autre rêve, il vit.

The Captain Is Getting Married

CENDRINE, HER LIPS PURSED, HER EYELIDS SMARTING FROM TOO MANY sleepless nights, carefully pulls her needle through. A garland of orange blossoms starts at the neck of the dress, lingers at the belt as bouquets, and runs in spirals to the bottom of the skirt.

Rich embroidery on a beautiful fabric. This working woman hasn't been concerned either about how much effort it took or how much it cost. For almost fifteen years now she has been saving up her coins for her bridal outfit and decided on the style she wanted.

As the evening angelus sounds, she makes the final stitches. Her shoulders are hurting, her temples are buzzing. But she joyfully makes the sign of the cross. She has finished her work.

She pulls a lounge chair next to the casement window and stretches out for a moment.

Outside, a remnant of daylight lingers on the plumes of the coconut trees rustling on the beach. The sand grows dark. The bronze tones of the little islands become tinged with violet.

In the sky, golds and purples remain in the spot where the sun sank out of sight. In the distance, where the indigo of the sea is drowned little by little in the night, Cendrine watches as a long fringe of white foam approaches the water's edge.

One of her neighbors is leaning on her elbows at the window in her usual way.

"Well, Cendrine, the big day is nearly here!"

"Oh yes, only a week more!"

"So much the better, girl, you've been very patient."

She has been waiting for fifteen years. Brisefer travels throughout the Caribbean. From time to time, on his stopovers, he scribbles a few lines. Every two or three years, he shows up unexpectedly. For a week, Cendrine is happy and filled with joy, basking in his dear presence. In between his amazing sailor's tales, he mutters words of fierce tenderness in his warm voice. Then the sea takes her husband-to-be away once more. Once again alone in her shack, shaded by coconut palm trees, Cendrine looks after her brood of ducklings.

Every now and again a woman pushes open the door. She unwraps her madras. She spreads out lengths of nainsook cotton on the table. Her children need shirts. Cendrine turns the material over and over in her hands. With her expert eye, she estimates what it would make.

The client is an old acquaintance—a young woman from the same neighborhood, an old playmate or Sunday school friend, now a housewife. She talks nonstop, singing the praises of her brood.

"Paulo, y'know, is already running around like a rabbit. He knows all of his brothers' names. At fifteen months!"

Cendrine smiles, dreamily.

"And you, my dear? Tell me. What about the captain?"

Her cheeks darkening a little, the young woman opens her keepsake chest. A few trinkets! A pearl fan, some little wicker baskets, old lace handkerchiefs . . . A handful of letters and postcards, with stamps from all the ports of the Caribbean and other places. Surinam . . . Port-of-Spain . . . Maracaibo, etc.

Now, all of that is in the past!

Brisefer is back, and for good. He will be coming any moment now, and will plant himself in this armchair, right next to her, and will court her like a seaman—both shy and blunt, excited and silent, tender and gruff.

Cendrine doesn't feel tired anymore. She braids her hair in heavy plaits, rolls them up, and pins them up with large, solid tortoiseshell combs. She perfumes her hands with a sprig of vetiver, adds a little powder to her cheeks, and decks herself out in a long white "gole," with lace ruffles at the collar and cuffs.

She gives the room a quick tidying up. The bits of wire and fabric disappear. The woman in love arranges the chairs carefully, and then sits down, her ears pricked.

What a stroke of luck that the *Bonne-Mère* has been laid up! It has just been condemned, consigned to the graveyard for old tubs. According to Brisefer, his career could not continue. The ship was listing tremendously, taking on water more and more.

Too bad for the captain, but just great for the bride-to-be, since he has come back to his village and the date for the marriage has finally been set.

On Sunday, at the parish mass, the third and final public notification will be given.

On the beach, the skipper of the *Rénette*, an old friend, calls out to Brisefer.

"So, Captain, you've dropped anchor?"

Brisefer, sitting astride the keel of an overturned boat, offers his hand absentmindedly. His eyes are fixed on the horizon.

A ship is in sight on the port side of the sandbanks. The two sailors watch it, their eyes intense. One pipe goes out.

"Want a light?"

"Go ahead!"

They bring their heads together, their clay pipes touching. The tobacco glows. Enveloped in a pungent cloud of smoke, the men wander off, going back toward the sea.

The schooner brig tacks. The jibs are inflated and it starts to move. The *Rénette*'s skipper continues, in a teasing tone:

"The wedding's on Saturday, right, bro'?"

"Yes, it's taken me a long time, but I've got there just the same."

"Indeed," Cirba jokes, "a sailor on land is like a rider without a horse. When you don't have the decks under your feet, the only thing you're good for is to do something foolish."

Without showing that the blow has struck home, Brisefer exclaims:

"What a fine brig! Do you know what port it's out of?"

"No, I don't. The factory is expecting struts from Norway and an engine from Surinam."

A strong breeze causes the pennant at the top of the mainmast to unfurl. The two men salute it with equal enthusiasm.

Shading their eyes with their hands, they make their way in the direction of the ship that is sailing toward the Caravelle.

They walk along the coast in a line parallel to the brig, criticizing the way it is being maneuvered. When the rocks at the tip of the headland prevent them from going any further they turn back with regret. Abruptly, Brisefer leans on Cirba's shoulder:

"She's really a very nice girl, right?"

"Cendrine? Why, yes, of course!"

"So I'm right, buddy! At the age of forty, it's time to dump ballast. And then we should each take turns to take a wife, to get dolled up, eh, old pal!

But Cirba isn't listening any longer. A whistle from the factory summons him back to his post. The crew from the *Rénette* are preparing to load barrels of tafia. The trucks are ready. The mules, harnessed one in front of the other between the rails, cock their ears nervously. At a click of the tongue they set off with short steps towards the wharf, where empty canoes are rocking on the water line. Cirba checks in.

Brisefer, left alone, a spyglass in his hand, sketches figures in the sand. One, two, three heads of children . . . Is it too late? He is getting a little white at the temples, but his hair is still thick, his eyes still clear, his feet nimble.

Too late? Certainly not. A new life is opening in front of him.

All of a sudden, he straightens up and makes his way, with a dashing gait and whistling, to the house where Cendrine is waiting for him.

Tomorrow is the wedding. Aunts, great uncles, cousins, and friends will be arriving from the surrounding heights.

The sexton is trimming the shrubs lining the driveway leading to the church. Inside, everything is ready. All the gold is shining. Altar cloths are changed. Brand new candles rise up in front of the alcove where the Virgin Mary is smiling.

At the entrance to the city hall the janitor shakes out the rugs. The entire village seems to be celebrating. Old Cirba's wife is lovingly ironing his best white shirt for him, a "milli-pleat" shirt. The women bustle importantly around Cendrine, each chattering louder than the other. The bride-to-be is busy, making decisions about table linens, handing out dish towels, bringing out the silverware and the provisions, and she is everywhere, supervising everything.

"Cousin Cendrine, can you just show us your wedding gown?"

It's made of fine lawn, and trimmed with imitation Valenciennes lace. The young country girls admire it, their mouths agape.

The bridesmaids, feverish with excitement, sew cascades of ribbons onto their sky-blue dresses. They put flowers in the cool and curl the lace on their clutch bags.

In the kitchen, there is a lot of commotion. Césarine, a neighbor, twists the neck of the largest duck. Another neighbor skins a white rabbit.

Brisefer slips away, irritated by the comings and goings of all the folks present, their numbers increasing by the hour. He perches on a rocky point at the edge of an inlet and inhales the sea air that is heavy with marine scents.

His thoughts are on the *Bonne-Mère*. It's been in dry dock for how many weeks now? He counts on his fingers. Only six? That's not possible! So it hasn't been months and months? How slow time passes on dry land! Once he is married, he will try to get a new schedule, for short trips, of course . . .

What's the use of fooling himself! Short or long, you can't pick and choose. All the ships of any significance have officers. No position . . . Unless some old sea wolf decides to retire.

Until that happens, Brisefer, captain of the *Bonne-Mère*, a laid-up schooner, will be carving little boats for his sons out of empty coconut shells. He will be dreaming, looking out onto a Caribbean sea filled with gliding sailboats.

His memory is haunted by these schooners, their hulls groaning in the wind, stylish, graceful, dressed up like girls about to get married, or tired of knocking about . . .

Marie-Joseph, his first command . . . *Anabelle*, all white, with tall sails and an elegant cut of the jib . . . taking the water so valiantly in any weather. And poor *Dora-Lise*, which sank one night near Sabbat . . . A hellish passage . . . And right up to the last one, this *Bonne-Mère*, so light in the breeze, despite its damaged hull.

He remembers the *Roxelane*, more beautiful, more impressive than all the others. One day he passed it off the coast of Cayenne. But fast as an arrow, it outran the *Bonne-Mère* by a good couple of hours.

After dropping anchor, the captains hailed one another on the megaphones and invited each other to visit their tubs.

Brisefer remembers that for a whole week he didn't sleep. What a schooner, my friends! You don't find any of that class anymore, since those damned steamboats have gradually displaced the sailboats. What captain wouldn't give up his share of paradise for one such command!

But the *Roxelane* is far away! And Brisefer's ambitions are dead.

Tomorrow, a new life . . .

"Here you are at last, Captain. I've been looking for you all over the village for at least an hour."

"What do you want with me, little one?"

"A registered letter addressed to you. Sign here."

Surprised, the man turns the envelope over between his fingers. Where did it come from? It doesn't matter much to him! Some prank by an old buddy who heard about his getting married. That was the custom among seamen.

Brisefer slips the letter into his pocket, takes out his pipe and lights it. His eyes on the far horizon, he takes some slow puffs.

Time passes; he has to go back in for lunch.

Suddenly, his hands find the envelope, which he had forgotten. He opens it.

A sheet with a letterhead . . . The name of a ship owner . . . The old sea dog's lips start to tremble . . . His sight becomes blurred.

Controlling his excitement, he reads aloud. Is it possible, he is being summoned over there. They are offering him, Brisefer, command of the *Roxelane*.

That can't be so! This is a joke, a cruel hoax dreamt up by his pals the day before his wedding!

Yet, this letter, delivered officially by mail, this stamp from Guyana, this postmark, this signature . . . are authentic.

It's difficult for the captain to repress an urge to scream for joy. Could it be that once again, he could be free on the sea, facing the sun, in the midst of sea spray and wind? Master on board, after God . . . And aboard . . . the *Roxelane*!

What is he waiting for to make up his mind, to hurry to the port? He has to leave, without delay. What's the date today? Isn't the liner for Cayenne due to weigh anchor this very evening? Oh! To leave, to leave! To reach Fort-de-France by any means possible! To arrive in time . . . To take the boat!

He hurtles down the slope, distraught.

There is a coach stopped outside the factory. Passengers are getting off. Suitcases are being unloaded.

"Hey! Partner! Are you going back to town?"

"Right away, if that's what you want!

Without a word, Brisefer settles into the back of the coach. It goes through the village, as if launched like a rocket.

He estimates his chances of arriving in time. Just enough time! Imagine that he is at the mercy of some kind of stupid breakdown!

Go fast! Faster than that!

Before his eyes he can already see the schooner's sails being unfurled, sparkling in the light bathing the Caribbean.

A white silk dress, finely embroidered with orange blossom flowers, which he once saw, in another dream, vanishes into oblivion.

Les Deux Carrés de Larammée

Maintenant que voici les lampes allumées, c'est bien volontiers que je vous dirai mon conte. Autrement si je m'y risquais en plein jour, savez-vous à quoi je m'exposerais? Ni plus ni moins qu'à me transformer sur l'heure en «panier».

N'importe qui vous le jurerait ici. A ma place, là devant vous, il n'y aurait plus qu'un petit panier de paille. Vide. Mais oui, je serais «tournée en panier» sur l'heure.

Chacun le sait aussi et vous le dira, au besoin. Au temps où le diable encore gamin en culottes courtes jouait au cerf-volant dans les savanes, pour nous, la vie était pur contentement. Elle baignait dans la joie. Comme le sel dans l'eau de la mer ou la fraîcheur dans le vent du soir.

Quel bien-être pour les yeux, les oreilles, toujours! Rien que des sourires sur les visages! Des rires, de la musique dans toutes les voix! Des mots aimables sur toutes les lèvres, dans la bouche des jeunes, des vieux!

Que dis-je, les bouches? Mais les becs aussi, et les museaux, et les groins mêmes . . . Puisque tous les êtres vivants avaient la parole. Les animaux, de l'éléphant et la baleine au moustique, à la sardine . . . Plus, revêtus de poils, de plumes, d'écailles . . . qu'ils courent ou qu'ils volent! que privés de pattes et d'ailes, ils ne sachent que nager ou ramper!

Tous, je vous le dis, parlaient, et en vérité, se comprenaient usant d'un même unique langage.

Bien mieux, entre les arbres, les plantes et les herbes . . . entre les eaux, et l'air et le vent régnaient entente et constante bonne humeur . . . Puisque partout demeurait l'harmonie. C'était paix. C'était fête . . . qu'hélas vint à troubler qui ou quoi?

On dit, mais j'ai peine à le croire, que l'enfant diable ayant grandi—et mal tourné—avec les ans, s'amusa à pervertir d'abord ses anciens camarades de jeu. Les hommes auraient découvert l'ennui . . . L'envie, les disputes, la discorde, la colère, la haine surgirent du même coup. Et, puisque tracé, le mauvais exemple, s'imposa aux animaux, aux lianes, aux sources, à la brise elle-même.

D'où les excès d'humeur, les affrontements . . . les orages . . . cyclones, volcans et tous les cataclysmes dits naturels, en constante menace depuis.

Dispersés, divisés, les vivants se groupèrent en clans ennemis. Et la langue commune disparut. Puisqu'entre voisins on demeurait sourd, on se tenait dos à dos—point n'était besoin de se comprendre.

Autant de familles, autant de langages désormais.

Il s'établit une telle confusion, qu'aux choses et aux animaux, pour commencer, la parole fut enlevée, en manière d'avertissement, à la folie de l'espèce humaine. Qui, des vivants, en fut privé pour commencer? On l'ignore. On croit seulement savoir quand, en quelles circonstances, vint le tour du bonhomme Chien.

Aussi, je ne garantis rien. Je ne tiens l'histoire ni de mon grand-père, ni même du grand-père de mon grand-père. On la doit aux plus anciens de nos anciens.

Mais vous avez, comme moi, déjà vu de très vieux murs en ruines dans la campagne martiniquaise? Au hameau «St. Jacques» par exemple? De gros paquets de pierres grises, meulées par le vent et les pluies, ficelées par d'énormes racines à nœuds, moisies, on dirait un entrelac de serpents à peau tachetée.

C'était exactement ce qui restait de la grande maison du très très vieux «Monsieur».

Une vieille maison bâtie dans une île aujourd'hui disparue. Aucune carte au monde n'en porte trace. On prétend qu'elle ressemblait trait pour trait à notre Martinique. Pourquoi ne serait-ce pas la même? La Martinique, pardi, au temps où elle barbotait dans l'est-atlantique, au bord du continent africain!

Elle serait partie en balade? Les courants l'ont poussée disent les uns! C'est la faute aux cyclones avancent les autres.

Venue par eau ou par air, la voici bel et bien à présent, miette d'Afrique paradant en pleine mer Caraïbe. Et pour en faire preuve, les vestiges de la grande maison du très très vieux Monsieur. Qui il était?

Père-Amour il s'appelait. Avait le teint pareil au bois de courbaril, des yeux brillants dans sa face sombre, encadrée du blanc de sa barbe et d'une chevelure épaisse, crépue comme coton cardé.

On dit qu'il se tenait droit sur des jambes solides tel un homme au plein de sa force . . . et puis que tous lui témoignaient un extrême respect. Au point que personne, absolument personne n'élevait la voix en sa présence. C'était à lui de parler le premier.

Pourtant, affable, il aimait s'arrêter, prêter l'oreille en bavardant avec tous, indistinctement.

Père-Amour, on lui disait, en deux mots presque familiers, tant qu'il souriait. Mais, au premier froncement de sourcils, on s'empressait de lui donner du «Monsieur Bon Dieu».

Car c'était Lui, le Bon Dieu, en personne! Pourquoi pas? Puisque la terre en son entier lui appartient, il s'y trouve également chez lui en tous lieux.

Quitter les anges et les Saints du Paradis pour faire un petit tour ailleurs, ça peut l'amuser, non? Enfin ça a pu l'amuser en ce temps-là, de venir en vacances dans sa maison de l'île minuscule, en plein bleu du plus chaud de l'Atlantique. Il s'y plaisait sans doute. S'il ne s'y montre plus c'est peut-être que nos querelles l'en dissuadent.

Déjà au moment de mon histoire les choses se gâtaient entre ses créatures. Les hommes se toléraient les uns les autres de moins en moins. Quant aux animaux, attentifs à les imiter dans leur comportement, ils ne s'amélioraient pas. Se mesurant, ils s'affrontaient soi-disant pour rire mais coups de griffes, de dents, de cornes, rageurs causaient fréquemment de graves plaies.

Il fallait toutes sortes de compresses et d'onguents pour réparer les dégâts.

—Puisqu'ils ne savent pas se modérer, déclara le Père-Amour, il me faut leur enseigner le moyen de parer au mal qu'ils se font.

Et Dieu s'en vint ainsi à révéler aux bêtes, aux gens, les vertus curatives des matières, des plantes, des eaux, éparses dans la nature. Il leur apprit comment effacer les ecchymoses, réduire les entorses, par exemple à partir des feuilles de giraumont ou d'aloès . . . comment guérir une morsure avec les poils même du chien coupable. Et cent et mille recettes encore en usage aujourd'hui.

A se les transmettre de bouche à oreille on en fit des mises en garde, des conseils qui devinrent nos premiers proverbes.

On vous en sert à tout propos au cours de la conversation en Martinique campagnarde. Il en reste de très vieux tel ce «pouèl chien gueri mossu chien».

D'autres, récentes trouvailles de malappris, se révèlent contraires à l'esprit du Père-Amour. Témoin le «Chaque luciole fait brûler veilleuse pour son propre salut» exaltant l'égoïsme.

La tribu chien eut, la première, à réfléchir sur un des plus sages dictons:
«tout mangé bon pou mangé
toute parole pas bon pou dit»
«Toute nourriture est bonne à prendre, non pas toute parole bonne à dire»
On était à la veille de Noël.

Toby chien, musicien hors ligne, avait passé l'après-midi à faire répéter une dernière fois des cantiques à la chorale qu'il dirigeait. Au crépuscule il partit comme tous les soirs en promenade avec le Pére-Amour dont il était un peu le compagnon préféré.

Les outils sur l'épaule, les paysans rentrant du travail croisaient les promeneurs.

—Courage! Courage les enfants! leur lançait le Père-Amour, la main levée pour les bénir.

On se souhaite bon courage au lever ainsi qu'au coucher du soleil aux Antilles. C'est façon courante de se saluer.

Ce soir-là, comme d'habitude, passa le vieux Larammée. Tout cassé de fatigue, Larammée. Il ne portait sur l'épaule ni coutelas, ni houe relativement légers, mais un mayombé. C'est-à-dire la lourde fourche à quatre dents qu'il faut plonger avec force dans la terre à labourer, rouge et grasse à souhait, pour l'en arracher ensuite.

Dieu s'arrêta, et comme tous les soirs, demanda au paysan:

—«Qui nove, Larammée? (Quoi de neuf?) Comment marche ton travail?»

—Piam . . . piam, monsieur Bon Dieu. (Couci-couça)

—Et quand espères-tu l'achever?

A quoi Larammée répondit comme chaque fois:

—«Demain! Monsieur Bon Dieu! Demain!»

Leur dialogue s'engageait et s'achevait invariablement ainsi tous les soirs. Sur les mêmes mots. Larammée avait entrepris de remuer au mayombé deux «carrés» de terre à manioc.

Ça aussi, vous le savez? Qu'on parle chez nous de «carrés» de terre, comme on parle ailleurs de parcelle, d'arpents ou d'acres.

Mais, plus il travaillait et plus il restait de terre à labourer à Larammée. C'est à croire que les «carrés» de son champ se multipliaient avec le temps.

Le pauvre homme espérait chaque jour en finir le soir même. Et chaque soir il espérait vivre le lendemain sa dernière corvée de mayombé.

Chaque soir Père-Amour déçu s'éloignait sans commentaire aucun. Cette fois, il en parla à Toby:

—Demain! Demain! Si seulement Larammée s'avisait que ce n'est pas à lui d'en décider! » dit-il un peu bougon.

Or le lendemain, une surprise l'attendait. Quand il rencontra Larammée et lui posa la question coutumière:

—«Quand espères-tu achever ton ouvrage?»

Larammée, l'air finaud répliqua:

—«Demain! S'il plaît à Dieu.» en insistant sur les derniers mots.

Une fois encore Dieu s'éloigna sans rien ajouter. Il ne fit aucune observation à Toby qui, trahissant sa confiance, avait pris l'initiative de prévenir le paysan.

Toby d'ailleurs, l'air gêné, le suivait à petite distance, n'osant pas sauter et gambader comme d'habitude, en quête d'une caresse. Le silence du Maître l'inquiétait. Il lui fallait s'expliquer. La langue lui démangeait de reprendre la conversation si amicale d'ordinaire. Il se sentait des picotements dans la gorge. N'y tenant plus, Toby, sur le chemin du retour, enfreignant la discipline habituellement observée, voulut s'exclamer:

—Père-Amour!

Stupeur! A la place des sons articulés on entendit:

—Ouah! Ouah! Ouah! Des cris! Des cris! et encore des cris! Il ne lui sortait que des jappements de la gorge!

Le chien faillit s'étrangler d'émotion . . . Plus encore lorsque, tout doucement, en lente et ferme poussée la langue vint à lui passer entre les dents. Sa langue, comme trop volumineuse, trop longue pour trouver place sous son palais lui sortait de la bouche.

Plus Toby essayait de s'expliquer et plus les sons devenaient vagues, et plus s'allongeait sa langue lamentablement, vilainement étalée devant lui, en bavoir.

Sur la pelouse de la grande maison le reste de la famille chien attendait.

Désastre! Au lieu des joyeux compliments de bienvenue, on n'entendit plus, en réponse aux premiers mots du Maître, que des ouah! ouah! oauh! oauh! oauh! oauh! à tous les échos! Une insoutenable cacophonie!

Dans l'impossibilité de s'exprimer à son habitude, chacun se démenait, donnait de la voix, bondissait, agitait furieusement la queue, poussait des cris, et des cris. Aboyait, et aboyait de plus belle.

Haut dans le ciel, l'étoile du berger s'allumait, annonçant Noël.

Il n'y aurait pas de chorale. Ni ce soir là. Ni plus jamais.

Noël! Une fête manquée . . . Morte désormais pour les chiens qui s'en souviennent encore. Une fête du temps révolu qu'ils regrettent au long des rêves qui agitent leur sommeil.

Lorsque, la tête et le cou entre les pattes, ils dorment, secoués de tressaillements, poussant des plaintes brèves, c'est qu'ils revivent le passé. Mais pas forcément en déplorant, pour eux-mêmes, l'usage perdu de la parole.

Depuis longtemps ils en ont pris leur parti. Depuis longtemps, ils ont appris à s'exprimer autrement. Par le regard, la caresse du front, l'agitation des oreilles et de la queue, ils excellent à manifester la confiance et l'attachement qu'ils gardent au grand frère, l'homme.

S'il leur faut faire effort pour comprendre la conversation courante en longues phrases détaillées, ils saisissent au moins le sens général de notre discours. Réduits en onomatopées familières. D'accord? Mais n'interprètent-ils pas nos grognements, nos réactions de joie, de crainte, et jusqu'à nos silences? Ne leur arrive-t-il pas de flairer le danger, de nous en prévenir?

En l'absence du Père commun, le vieil homme aux cheveux blancs, ils s'entretiendraient encore avec vous, s'ils en avaient le moyen. Pour nous rappeler à l'occasion les préceptes de sagesse dont ils se souviennent . . . Retenir par exemple tel bavard sur le point d'oublier que «Toute parole n'est pas bonne à dire, si toute nourriture bonne à prendre».

Au lendemain de ce jour de Noël, la dernière fête consentie par le Père-Amour à la grande maison de l'île, Larammée parvint à bout de sa tâche.

Son champ, enfin, retournée, entièrement labouré comme par enchantement. Il se souvint de la leçon. Il l'enseigna sans hésiter aux voisins, aux amis. Plus jamais un paysan martiniquais n'a annoncé, depuis n'annonce et n'annoncera le plus anodin des projets sans ajouter un prudent «S'il plait à Dieu».

Pas un seul ne s'aviserait d'affirmer «Je verrai, ou ferai ou accomplirai ceci ou cela demain.» Demain? Demain tout court? Jamais!

Sur ce, il me faut prendre congé mes amis, au revoir! A demain . . . à une autre fois, à l'an qui vient, au prochain Noël . . . S'il plaît à Dieu!

Larammée's Two Squares

Now that the lights are on, I'd be happy to tell you my story. Otherwise, if I took the chance to do so in the daytime, do you know what I would be exposing myself to? Nothing more or less than being transformed at once into a "basket."

Anyone here would swear to you that that's true. Here in front of you where I am standing, there would be only a small straw basket. Empty. Oh yes, I would be "turned into a basket" instantly.

Everybody knows it too and would tell you, if need be: At the time when the devil was still a kid in short pants, playing with his kite on the open fields, life for us was pure contentment. Life was a constant bath of joy. Like salt in seawater or the coolness in the evening wind.

What a treat for the eyes and the ears, all the time! Nothing but smiles on people's faces! Laughter and music in everybody's voice! Friendly words on everyone's lips, in the mouths of young and old!

What am I saying, mouths? But beaks too, and muzzles, and even snouts . . . Because all living creatures had speech. Animals, from the elephant and the whale to the mosquito, to the sardine . . . those covered in fur, in feathers, in scales . . . whether they ran or flew! . . . whether they had no paws or wings, whether they could only swim or crawl!

Everyone, I tell you, could speak, and in truth, everyone understood one another using the same and only language.

Even better, among trees, plants, and grasses . . . among the waters, and the air and the wind, there reigned agreement and a constant good mood

. . . Because there was harmony everywhere. There was peace; there was a nonstop celebration . . . But, alas, who or what came to disturb it?

They say, although I have a hard time believing it, that the young devil, who had grown up and turned bad over the years, amused himself by first corrupting his former playmates. Men had discovered boredom . . . Envy, quarreling, conflict, anger, and hate arose at the same time. And once bad example began, it spread to animals, to vines, to springs, to the breeze itself.

As a result, outbursts of temper, confrontations, storms, hurricanes, volcanoes, and all the cataclysms that we say are natural, became a constant threat thereafter.

Living beings, now dispersed and divided, formed groups of rival clans. And the common language disappeared. Since, though we were neighbors, we refused to listen to one another and turned our backs to one another, there was no need to understand one another.

From that time on, there were as many languages as families.

Such confusion developed, that first of all speech was taken away from things and animals, as a kind of warning of the madness of the human race. Who were the first living creatures to be deprived of speech? We do not know. The only thing we think we know is when and in what circumstances it was Mister Dog's turn.

Also, I can't vouch for anything. I did not get this story from my grandfather, or even from my grandfather's grandfather. It comes from the eldest of our elders.

But have you, as I have, already seen very old walls in ruin in Martinique's countryside? In the "St. Jacques" hamlet, for example? Large packs of grey stones, ground by wind and rain, and tied together by huge, knotted, rotten roots that look like snakes with spotted skins intertwined.

That was exactly what was left of the great house of the very very old "Mister."

An old house built on an island that today has disappeared. There is no trace of it on any map in the world. They claim that it looked in every feature like our Martinique. Why wouldn't it be the same island? Martinique, by gosh, at the time when it dabbled in the eastern Atlantic, beside the African continent!

Could it be that Martinique took a stroll? The currents pushed it, some people say! Others suggest that it was the hurricanes that did it.

Whether it came by water or by air, here it is now, a crumb of Africa parading right in the middle of the Caribbean sea. And to prove it, the ruins of the great house of the very very old Mister. Who was he?

Father-Love was his name. His complexion was just like jatoba wood.* He had shining eyes in a dark face, framed by the white of his beard and thick hair, frizzy like card cotton.

They say that he carried himself upright on strong legs like a man in the fullness of his strength, and that everyone treated him with extreme respect. To the point that no one, absolutely no one, raised their voice in his presence. It was up to him to speak first.

Yet, he was sociable and liked to stop and lend an ear and chat with any- and everyone.

Father-Love, they called him, using the two words. In an almost casual way, when he was smiling. But, at the first sign of a frown, they would quickly address him as "Mr. God."

Because it was He—God, in person! And why not? Since earth in its entirety belongs to him, he finds himself at home everywhere on it.

Leaving the angels and the saints of heaven to take a stroll somewhere else could be fun, couldn't it? Well, it must have amused him in those days to come on vacation to his house on this miniscule island, in the deep blue of the hottest place in the Atlantic. No doubt he liked it there. If he doesn't show up there anymore, maybe it is because our squabbles put him off.

At the time of my story, things were already starting to turn bad among his creatures. People tolerated one another less and less. And as for the animals, careful as they were to imitate humans in their behavior, they were not getting better. Comparing themselves one to the other, they fought, apparently in fun, but furious strokes of claws, teeth, and horns frequently caused serious injuries.

All sorts of compresses and ointments were needed to fix the damages.

"Since they do not know how to behave," declared Father-Love, "I need to teach them how to deal with the harm they are causing one another."

And so God came to reveal to animals and to people the curative qualities of things, in plants and waters, found here and there in nature. He taught them how to make bruises fade, how to fix sprains, by using, for example, pumpkin leaves or aloes . . . how to heal a bite with the hair of the dog that bit. And a thousand and one remedies still being used today.

By passing these remedies on by word of mouth to one another, we made them into warnings, bits of advice that became our first proverbs.

We use them on any subject in conversations in rural Martinique. Some very old ones still remain, such as "Dog hair heal dog bite."

Others, recent ones coined by people who don't know any better, turn out to be the opposite of what Father-Love had in mind. For instance, "Every firefly burns a nightlight to keep himself safe" exalts selfishness.

The dog tribe was the first to reflect on one of the wisest sayings: "All food good to eat, but all words not good to say."

It was Christmas Eve.

Toby, a dog, and a top class musician, had spent the afternoon holding a final rehearsal of canticles with the chorus he directed. At dusk, he left as he did every night to walk with Father-Love, whose favorite companion he was.

Peasants coming home from work with their tools on their shoulders crossed the path of the two walkers.

"Take heart! Take heart, children!," Father-Love would say, lifting his hand to bless them.

In the French Caribbean we tell one another to take heart at the rising as well as at the setting of the sun. It is a common way to greet one another.

That evening, as usual, old Larammée passed by. He was completely exhausted, was Larammée. On his shoulder he carried not a cutlass or a hoe, which would have been relatively light, but a "mayombé." That is a heavy four-prong fork that needs to be driven with force into the soil to be ploughed, as red and lush as one could wish, and then pulled out.

God stopped, and, as he did every night, asked the peasant: "What's up, Larammée? How is your work going?"

"So-so, Mr. God."

"And when are you hoping to finish it?"

To which Larammée replied, as he did every time: "Tomorrow, Mr. God! Tomorrow!"

Their dialogue started and ended in exactly this way every evening. With the same words. Larammée's job was to fork up two "squares" for planting cassava.

That's another thing. Did you know that here we talk about "squares" of ground, just as in other places they talk about plots, or arpents, or acres? But the more he worked, the more ground was left for Larammée to plough. It was as if the "squares" of his field multiplied with time.

Every day the poor man hoped to finish that evening, and every evening he hoped the next day would be his last mayombé task.

Every night Father-Love walked away disappointed, without making any comment. This time, he talked about it to Toby: "Tomorrow! Tomorrow! If only Larammée realized that it is not up to him to decide!," he said a little grumpily.

The next day, however, he was in for a surprise. When he met Larammée and asked him the usual question: "When do you hope to finish your work?," Larammée replied, with a crafty look on his face: "Tomorrow! God willing," stressing the last words.

Once again, God moved away without saying anything. He made no comment to Toby, who had betrayed his confidence and had taken the initiative to warn the peasant.

Toby, on the other hand, was apparently embarrassed and followed a little distance behind him, not venturing to jump and leap as he usually did, looking to be petted. The Master's silence worried him.

He needed to explain himself. His tongue was itching to resume the cordial conversation they usually had. He felt stinging sensations in his throat. As they walked back, Toby couldn't stand it anymore and wanted to break the discipline they usually observed and exclaim: "Father-Love!"

What a shock! Instead of articulated sounds, all that could be heard was: "Woof! Woof! Woof!" Shouts! Shouts! and more shouts! Nothing but yelps came out of his throat!

The dog almost choked with fright . . . Even more so when, very gently, slowly and firmly, his tongue pushed through his teeth. As if it were too bulky and too long to fit under his palate, his tongue came out of his mouth.

The more Toby tried to find an explanation for what was happening, the more muffled the sounds became, and the more his tongue extended pitifully, spreading out wickedly in front of him, like a bib.

On the lawn of the great house, the rest of the dog family was waiting for him.

What a disaster! Instead of joyful expressions of welcome, all that was heard, in response to the Master's first words, was "Woof! woof! woof! woof! woof! woof!" over and over again! An unbearable cacophony!

Each of them, not being able to express themselves in the usual way, thrashed about, made noise, leapt, and shook their tails furiously, letting out shout after shout. They barked and barked louder and louder.

High in the sky, the shepherd's star lit up, announcing Christmas.

There would be no choir. Not that night. Never again.

Christmas! A wasted holiday. Dead henceforth for dogs who still remember it—a holiday of times past that they regret in dreams that disturb their sleep.

When they sleep, with their head and neck between their paws, and shake with shudders, moaning from time to time, it is because they are reliving the past. But not necessarily grieving over their loss of speech.

A long time ago they took their stand. A long time ago, they learned to express themselves differently. With a look, a caress with their forehead, a shaking of the ears and the tail, they excel at demonstrating the trust and attachment they still have for their big brother, man.

If they have to struggle to understand a conversation that involves long, elaborate sentences, at least they get the general gist of what we are saying. Reduced to familiar onomatopoeias. Isn't that so? But don't they interpret our grumbling, our reactions of joy and fear, even our silences? Don't they smell danger and warn us of it?

Since the common Father is absent, the old man with white hair, they would still converse with us if they were able to. To remind us every once in a while of the precepts of wisdom that they remember . . . To restrain, for example, a talkative person who is on the verge of forgetting that "Every word is not good to say, even if all food is good to eat."

The day after that Christmas day, the last holiday allowed by Father-Love at the great house on the island, Larammée finished his task.

His field was finally forked up, completely ploughed as if by magic. He remembered the lesson. He did not hesitate to teach it to neighbors and friends. Never again did a Martinique peasant talk about doing even the most trivial thing without adding "God willing," and that's been the case ever since then and will be in the future.

Not one of them would think of stating, "I will see, or will do or finish this or that tomorrow." Tomorrow? Just tomorrow? Never!

At this point, I have to go, my friends. Goodbye! See you tomorrow . . . or another time, in the coming year, or next Christmas . . . God willing!

La Poupée de Son

On chuchote dans la forêt qu'au village il y a une petite poupée de son à l'œil vif, aux dents de porcelaine, au sourire heureux.

Tartine en main et sac au dos, elle part tous les matins pour l'école. C'est à qui lui tiendra compagnie. Tellement ses petites camarades la trouvent agréable.

Sa bonne vieille institutrice aussi l'affectionne très fort. «Une élève si bien douée et si gracieuse!» répète-t-elle à tous les échos.

Un après-midi de vacances, la petite poupée se promène dans la campagne. Le vent chante dans les branches. Les feuilles dansent. Un moment, la petite poupée danse avec la verdure des buissons.

Elle s'arrête dans une clairière. Va goûter à la fraîcheur d'une source. Des fourmis défilent dans l'herbe. «Bonjour! Voulez-vous qu'on bavarde un peu?»

À courir sans cesse dans le sous-bois, elles doivent en voir des choses, les fourmis! Malheureusement, elles sont toujours pressées. Elles bougonnent à peine un «Salut!» et s'éloignent.

Par chance, une mouche blonde est là qui regarde tranquillement, quoi? une araignée au travail. Extraordinairement habile, la fileuse! Elle tisse un immense parachute en filet très fin.

«Ce doit être amusant d'y faire un saut, dit la mouche. J'ai envie d'essayer.»

La petite poupée n'entend pas. Elle écoute la voix du ruisseau qui se cache dans un fossé. Comme il est charmant, le ruisseau! Il fait une couronne de bulles aux cailloux assis dans le sable.

Les pierres abritent des écrevisses, peut-être? La petite poupée suit le courant. Pour surprendre les écrevisses. Mais le ruisseau va loin. Et le bois est de plus en plus épais. La petite poupée marche tant et tant qu'elle s'égare entre les troncs. Une vraie forêt. Mais pas comme les autres. Une forêt enchantée.

Quand il fait nuit noire, la petite poupée, fatiguée, s'assied sous un champignon. Que faire, sinon, s'endormir à la belle étoile?

La petite poupée n'est pas peureuse, mais elle est bien contente de voir arriver une dame. Une fée, pour parler juste. Seulement ça ne se devine pas du premier coup.

Encore moins pourrait-on dire si elle est bonne ou méchante! Peut-être ni l'un ni l'autre? Qui sait? Pour le moment, elle s'arrête. Sourit à la petite poupée.

Les écureuils le savent bien que la dame a souvent l'air mauvais et les sourcils froncés. Ils se sauvent, prudents, quand elle passe. Dans le bois, on la connaît. On lui reproche, paraît-il, de manquer de cœur. Du moins d'avoir un cœur tellement étroit qu'il ne s'y trouve guère de place. Guère de place que pour un seul amour. Tout juste celui qu'elle a pour . . . elle-même. Mais oui, elle n'aime que sa propre personne!

Hélas, tout dort déjà, ce soir, aux alentours. Personne ne peut souffler à l'oreille de la petite poupée les noms et surnoms de la fée.

«Dame Toutamoi», l'appellent les uns. «Dame Cœur-de-Glace», lui disent d'autres. Comme elle aime bien se plaindre, certains la nomment parfois le «Crocodile» ou «Larmozieu».

Crocodile? Larmozieu? Allons donc! Avec ce sourire, elle est belle, la dame! Et charmante! Elle emmène facilement la petite poupée ensommeillée, si lasse déjà.

Le lendemain au réveil, la petite poupée se remet mal de sa surprise. Elle ne reconnaît ni la chambre, ne le lit. Pas plus que le visage de l'étrangère penchée sur elle.

Où est-elle? Pour quelles raisons? Que lui est-il arrivé? Quand? Comment? Plus elle se pose de questions et plus sa mémoire se trouble. Qui elle est, d'où elle vient? Elle ne le sait déjà plus. Elle oublie. Elle a tout oublié.

Le visage en face d'elle est plutôt agréable. Il rayonne de plaisir. Une nouvelle amie? Voilà qui fait chaud au cœur. La petite poupée rend sourire pour sourire. Elle croit la fée gentille et bonne.

Madame Toutamoi se répète tout bas que le hasard lui fait là un bien beau cadeau. Une mignonne poupée perdue, abandonnée de tous, en apparence, sans maman, sans amis pour la protéger. Une poupée qui a l'air naïf, et généreux, en plus!

Il faut profiter de l'aubaine! Madame Toutamoi n'y manquera pas. Désormais, la petite poupée sera sa servante, et rien d'autre. Une sorte de lutin, bon à tout faire. Et qui obéira! Quelques mots d'une formule dont elle a le secret, un coup de baguette magique, et hop! petit lutin s'activera! On l'appellera «Magiquette» d'abord.

Et Magiquette ne saura rien de ce que l'on attend d'elle. Pour commencer, elle aura la vie belle. Et tout lui sera permis. De se promener, de rêver dans le bois. D'aller libre comme une biche et de bavarder avec qui lui plaira.

Et de fait, bientôt grenouilles dans les mares, criquets dans les fourrés, merles dans les nids, abeilles autour de la ruche, tous deviennent ses amis.

Qu'on siffle, coasse, roucoule ou caquette autour d'elle, Magiquette comprend tout ce qui se dit. Et répond sans difficulté. C'est à qui lui contera une histoire, lui apprendra une chanson. Elle partage tous les jeux.

Aussi se prend-elle à aimer ses compagnons de plaisir, et leurs voisins, et leurs amis, et leurs cousins, et tout, et tous dans la forêt. Tous. Y compris madame Toutamoi.

Sortant et rentrant à sa fantaisie, Magiquette est la plus heureuse des petites poupées de son.

Au cours d'une promenade, un jour, elle croise une limace. La dame à la coquille va droit devant elle . . . puis elle revient sur ses pas . . . repart en avant, pour retourner de nouveau en arrière. Drôle de manège!

Magiquette s'arrête, intriguée. Elle n'ose questionner dame Limace. C'est la dame, plutôt bavarde, qui parle la première: «Tu n'es pas d'ici, toi?»

—Non Madame. Bonjour Madame.

—Pourquoi me dis-tu «Madame»? Dis-moi «Casodo» comme tout le monde. Ce sera plus gentil!

—Oui madame Casodo! Elles éclatent de rire en même temps. Et toute gêne disparaît entre elles.

—Comment t'appelles-tu, dis-moi?

—À présent, je suis Magiquette. Mon nom d'avant, je ne me le rappelle pas.

Son nom «d'avant». Elle en change donc? Casodo s'interroge, mais elle ne veut pas être indiscrète. Elle continue comme si de rien n'était:

—Pourquoi pas Magiquette? Ça ne sonne pas si mal! Puisqu'on se voit pour la première fois, Magiquette, j'arrête mon travail pour un moment. Pour fêter notre rencontre!

—Quel travail faites-vous là?

—Tu vois bien. Je mesure la distance d'une borne à l'autre sur le bord de la route.

«Quelles bornes?», se demande Magiquette. Elle n'en aperçoit aucune. Casodo explique:

—Le cantonnier-chef, c'est mon mari. Je lui marque l'emplacement des bornes tout en me promenant. Il vient ensuite les poser. Tu vas sûrement le rencontrer si tu vas par là. Pas difficile à reconnaître! Le bonhomme est plutôt obèse, malgré sa grande activité.

Un limaçon qui se démène beaucoup? Ça paraît bizarre à la petite poupée. Elle s'étrangle de rire. Un gros lourdaud qui s'agite comme un bourdon dans un bocal? Qui a déjà vu pareille chose?

De plus en plus bavarde, Casado poursuit:

—Mon fils casse des cailloux par là-bas d'où tu viens. Tu l'as vu au bord du chemin?

—Non. J'ai marché dans l'herbe. À travers champs.

—Alors tu n'as pas passé par le village des Insectes? Dommage! C'est aujourd'hui jour de marché!

Jour de marché? Au village des Insectes? Le cœur de Magiquette saute de joie! Il lui faut absolument voir cela. Se promener dans le village n'importe quel matin, ce doit être bien amusant. Mais y aller un jour de marché? Passionnant, en vérité!

Entre tous les spectacles vivants Magiquette aime celui du marché. Elle aime se mêler aux badauds. Elle aime écouter les camelots. Elle trouve beaux les étalages. Herbes, fruits, graines, feuilles, fleurs, rouges, verts, jaunes, rangés en tas sur les tables. On dirait des pans d'arc-en-ciel! De la joie en vente par tranches!

Et tellement amusants aussi parfois, les marchands! Plantés derrière leurs éventaires, on les voit rire. Se taquiner, se moquer gentiment les uns des autres. S'arrêter de babiller pour crier aux passants :

—Mes cerises, tout sucre, Mesdames! Et ma laitue? Pour rien aujourd'-hui, venez voir!

Même les clients sont amusants à regarder! Les dames surtout. On en voit de hardies qui plongent carrément dans le tas, palpent les fruits pour choisir les meilleures. D'autres, timides, hésitent. Elles tripotent leur porte-monnaie, comptent leurs sous, se tâtent les poches. Si seulement Casodo lui indiquait la direction à prendre, Magiquette se dépêcherait vers le marché!

Casodo s'ennuie probablement à travailler seule sur le bord de la route. Elle souhaite se reposer un peu, c'est entendu, mais Casodo a encore plus envie que quelqu'un l'écoute. C'est visible.

Heureusement, le ronron d'un moteur approche. Un camion! Au volant, un superbe scarabée.

Il s'arrête à la hauteur de la petite poupée toujours impatiente de se séparer de Casodo. Saluts. Sourires! Une place jusqu'au marché?

—Bien volontiers. C'est ma direction! Je vous descendrai à l'entrée du village des Insectes!

Scarabée fait une petite place à Magiquette. C'est la première fois que Magiquette passe en cet endroit. Elle a tout loisir d'admirer le paysage. Les arbres unissent leurs branches en arche au-dessus de la route. Magiquette est ravie. Le chauffeur, discret, ne lui adresse que très rarement la parole. Le temps file. Le soleil grimpe vite jusqu'au milieu du ciel.

Magiquette s'aperçoit en arrivant au village que de nombreux commerçants déjà commencent à plier bagage. Que de voitures! Le village et le marché sont encore plus importants que Magiquette ne l'imaginait.

Les stands sont de vraies boutiques. La marchandise souvent exposée dans de grandes voitures. Le capot s'ouvre sur de véritables rayons bien ordonnés.

«Sûrement, se dit Magiquette, les forains font des tournées dans tout le pays. Il faudra m'arranger pour savoir leurs différents jours de marché.»

En attendant, elle regarde de tous ses yeux. Dame Chenille tâte des salades. Dame Guêpe marchande des fruits. De robustes fourmis colportent des sacs bourrés de grains. Devant madame Libellule, flanquée de ses deux filles jumelles, dame Sauterelle, en blouse verte, attend. Elle a déroulé une coûteuse pièce de gaze devant la cliente. Dame Libellule, soucieuse, palpe l'étoffe.

«Pressons! Pressons!» signifie clairement le geste de madame Sauterelle. Elle fait impatiemment claquer ses gros ciseaux.

Magiquette court à la librairie. Là aussi on va fermer. Il est tard. Un monsieur vêtu de gris, un cloporte?, assis sur un banc à l'écart, attend sans doute que madame achève ses emplettes.

Sautillant sur un pied, Magiquette prend le chemin du retour. À travers bois de préférence. Quand elle arrive à la maison, madame Toutamoi est absente. Et Magiquette bien déçue. Elle a tant de choses à raconter! Et tant de joies à partager!

La dame revient enfin, et c'est pour Magiquette encore plus grande peine. Car la fée se dit souffrante. Par la faute de la petite poupée!

—Je sors de chez le médecin. Je te croyais perdue dans le bois et j'en étais malade de peur! Un malheur est si vite arrivé!

Le docteur m'a fait avaler des cachets. M'a donné des piqûres. Il me recommande le repos. Mais pas d'émotion.

—Il ne faudra plus vous inquiéter pour moi, propose Magiquette.

—Si tu étais gentille tu ne me quitterais pas trop souvent. Ni pour trop longtemps. Comme ça je serais tranquille!

Des promenades à jours fixes? Pour éviter du souci à son amie la fée? D'accord! Magiquette se décide pour les mardis, jeudis, samedis. Des jours de fête désormais pour elle. Le reste du temps, elle s'occupe à la maison comme une grande! Elle range, nettoie, lave, raccommode, et ne s'ennuie pas.

L'autre jeudi, Magiquette rentre au coucher du soleil, joyeuse comme une abeille et, comme une abeille, bourdonnante de bonnes nouvelles.

Elle s'est amusée en compagnie de jolies rainettes vertes. Trois petites cousines: Vivette, Viviane et Rennie, qui l'ont invitée à la baignade. L'eau était profonde, mais le lac tout petit. Un mignon petit lac tout rond «où le ciel se regarde et sourit tout le temps», disait Rennie.

Madame Toutamoi écoute, le sourcil froncé. Puis, elle ne reproche rien à Magiquette. Mais elle raconte à son tour.

Par hasard, juste aujourd'hui, elle a eu un malaise. Dieu merci, assez bref, mais qu'on ne s'est pas expliqué. Comment empêcher qu'il se reproduise? On n'en sait pas la cause!

Magiquette renonce d'elle-même à une sortie sur trois. En attendant que les choses s'arrangent.

Elles changent bien des choses, mais en mal. Les catastrophes s'entêtent à survenir en l'absence de la petite poupée. Il n'y a bientôt plus qu'un parti à prendre. Ne plus quitter la maison.

D'ailleurs la dernière sortie de Magiquette n'a pas été très gaie. Qui a-t-elle rencontré? Mansfrenil, tout noir comme un croque-mort. Mansfrenil le marin. Il a raconté une belle histoire de marin croyez-vous? Pas du tout. Le gros oiseau triste, le compère Gôh-Gôh qui crie sans cesse «J'ai soif! J'ai soif!», c'est de son aventure que Mansfrenil a parlé à Magiquette.

Vous savez, les sources, les rivières, les lacs et même les mares refusent leur eau à Gôh-Gôh. Cet oiseau ne peut boire que lorsqu'il tombe de la pluie. Parce que c'est un oiseau maudit. Maudit, oui. Pour avoir été méchant. Très méchant envers le Christ sur la croix.

«Je n'ai rien à me reprocher de pareil», se dit Magiquette. Il ne lui viendrait pas à l'idée de refuser un verre d'eau à qui que ce soit. Surtout pas à quelqu'un qui souffre, est blessé . . . A quelqu'un qui a les lèvres bleues . . . on ne passe pas une éponge mouillée de vinaigre sur la bouche! . . .

Non. Magiquette ne s'est pas trouvée dans ce cas. Jamais elle n'agirait de la sorte . . . Pourtant, elle réfléchit, la pauvre petite. Si c'était vrai que, sans le faire exprès, elle avait manqué de charité envers la fée? Si elle avait, par étourderie, négligé de faire un geste, un seul, de gentillesse et d'amitié juste au bon moment? De peur de causer un malheur, Magiquette prend une résolution. Elle ne s'éloignera plus de la maison. Ne sortira plus jamais pour son plaisir!

Et voilà! Les ruses de dame Toutamoi, l'hypocrisie de dame Crocodile ont gagné! Désormais Magiquette s'appliquera non seulement à obéir aux ordres de la fée, mais à deviner ses désirs. Hier encore, la dame avait-elle envie d'un sorbet, d'une délicieuse crème? Aussitôt, coup de baguette, formule magique! Et Magiquette devenait un vrai cordon bleu!

Fallait-il faire une friction? Préparer un cataplasme? «Pitté-patté-proutt

...et protté...!» Magiquette apparaissait en blouse et bonnet d'infirmière!

Et maintenant, la dame veut-elle une robe élégante? un châle pour les nuits fraîches, une chanson pour se distraire? «Pitté-patté-proutt»...

À peine les premiers mots prononcés, avant même que la baguette ne bouge, voici Magiquette taillant robe, tricotant châle, fredonnant refrain.

Alors, madame Toutamoi ne sait plus quoi inventer. Pour changer, elle se fait plaindre.

Heureuse de la soigner, de la consoler, Magiquette se montre de plus en plus zélée. De plus en plus attentive.

Un jour, piquée par un serpent venimeux, la fée se trouve en danger. Pour de bon. Elle n'a plus les pensées assez claires pour se rappeler les mots magiques. Et Magiquette n'est pas assez savante pour découvrir seule le remède qu'il faudrait.

Magiquette demande leur aide à ses amis de la forêt. Ils partent tous à la recherche d'herbes, de racines, d'écorces, pour composer onguents et tisanes de toutes sortes. Ils mettent la forêt sens dessus dessous. Consultent les anciens. Ils prennent conseil des sages. Rien n'y fait.

À la fin, Ara-Le-Vieux prend la parole:

—Nous avons employé tous les remèdes connus, mes amis. Il ne reste plus qu'à essayer un élixir enchanté pour tenter de sauver la malade. Je sais une recette... mais il faudrait puiser dans un cœur vivant... c'est très dangereux... Le donneur risque sa vie...

—Comment, s'écrie Magiquette, il ne faut que des forces vives, et vous hésitez?

Avant que l'on ne puisse l'en empêcher, la petite folle s'ouvre la poitrine. L'élixir est vite prêt. On le donne à madame Toutamoi.

Elle guérit. Par chance, Magiquette, se remet de sa blessure. Elle guérit aussi. Mais voici madame Larmozieu avec une nouvelle, une mauvaise habitude. Douleurs de reins, de jambes, de tête... elle se plaint de mille malaises nouveaux. Rien ne la soulage jamais qu'un cataplasme de son chaud.

Elle a sans cesse recours à Magiquette. Les bras, les muscles de la poupée se vident peu à peu. Bientôt la dame Cœur-de-glace n'attend pas d'avoir un prétexte pour se faire soigner. Elle en invente. Il suffit qu'elle souhaite, par exemple, de se «sentir bien en forme». Une fois, elle va jusqu'à réclamer du son «pour chasser les puces de son chien favori».

Et la dame fait tant et tant que Magiquette perd ses forces et sa vigueur. Plus la poupée s'affaiblit et plus le Crocodile, pleurant ou souriant, réclame du son. Encore et encore! Par plaisir.

Madame Toutamoi essaie un jour d'en arroser un bout de son jardin. Histoire de faire pousser des tomates bien rondes et des laitues bien pommées!

Magiquette supporte tout en secret. Elle ne se plaint à personne. Pourtant, ses amis s'inquiètent. Comme une fleur tranchée de sa tige, la petite poupée se fane. Elle se dessèche doucement.

«Il faut trouver de quoi renouveler ses forces. Et vite!» déclare Scarabée.

Il sillonne tout le pays à la recherche d'une médecine. Son gros camion passe par les chemins les plus difficiles.

Alertés une fois encore, tous les habitants de la forêt se consultent. Ils discutent sous un arbre vieux de plus de cent ans. Un catalpa géant.

Chacun dit ses craintes . . . donne son avis . . . offre son grain de sagesse.

Au cours de leurs nombreux voyages, les oiseaux, gros et petits, ont beaucoup vu et beaucoup retenu. Bien sûr. Mais les arbres? N'ont-ils pas pris le temps de faire des observations, de réfléchir longuement, des cent et des mille fois? Depuis les ans et les ans que, silencieux, immobiles, ils se recueillent et méditent!

La discussion générale est passionnée. Des bavards, comme chacun s'en doute, il y en a, parmi les oiseaux! À la fin, la voix du grand-père Catalpa domine toutes les autres:

«Aucun de nous ne sait pourquoi notre chère Magiquette a perdu la santé. Aucun de nous n'a pu découvrir le remède qui la guérirait. Mais si nous unissons nos forces, nous la sauverons!

Lorsque la vie s'épuise, c'est que le cœur s'épuise, oui ou non?»

Et tous de crier ensemble: «Tu dis vrai!»

«Que faut-il, pour rendre vigueur au cœur, dites, vous tous?»

Et tous de crier encore plus fort: «L'Amour! L'Amour!»

—Puisque c'est dans le cœur la force d'aimer, c'est dans le cœur la force de vivre!

—Tu dis vrais! tu dis vrai!

—Alors, écoutez, vous tous. Nous les grands arbres, nous enfonçons des racines dans la chair noire de la terre. Nous dressons la tête . . . Nous la plongeons dans le bleu du ciel. Nous sommes forts. Mais nous avons la vie en commun avec vous tous. Tous! les oiselets fragiles . . . les mouches aux ailes légères et les larves sans défense. Tous, du plus puissant au plus faible, nous sommes frères. Riches du même bien: la Vie. Et frères de Magiquette que nous aimons du même cœur.

«Alors, écoutez bien, vous tous. Et ceux dont le sang brûle rouge, et ceux dont la sève monte claire . . . Écoutez et jurez avec moi:

«En la durée du jour présent, nous sacrifions à Magiquette, notre sœur, ce qui nous tient le plus à cœur. Ce que nous aimons le plus au monde!»

D'une seule voix, tous répètent le serment à la suite de Catalpa. Tous. Madame Toutamoi comme les autres. «Qu'est-ce que je risque? pense-t-elle. Puisque je n'aime rien ni personne.»

En quoi elle se trompe. Pour parler juste, elle devrait préciser: «Je n'aime rien ni personne d'autre que moi-même.»

Voici comment madame Toutamoi fait une promesse, et prononce un serment qui l'engage dangereusement.

Voici comment se retourne contre elle son furieux, son terrible égoïsme. Comme elle n'aime que sa propre personne, c'est sa propre personne qu'elle vient d'engager. Et qu'elle condamne. Et qu'elle met en péril de mort.

Ce jour-là, chaque heure glissant au cadran, chaque heure ramène des roses aux joues de Magiquette. Et chaque heure voit se creuser une ride au cœur racorni de madame Toutamoi. Quand enfin, le soleil se couche sur la forêt, tous restent muets de surprise. Magiquette reprend vie et s'épanouit comme un bourgeon neuf au lever du soleil.

Madame Toutamoi, les yeux clos, garde la main ouverte auprès d'une baguette de bois mort.

Aucun des amis de Magiquette ne sait les mots de la formule magique qui réveillerait peut-être la dame évanouie . . . Ou rendrait son pouvoir à la baguette desséchée.

Même s'ils les savaient les mots secrets, souhaiteraient-ils s'en servir? Ils viennent de découvrir un secret beaucoup plus important. Il y a au monde une force dépassant toutes les autres, une magie plus puissante que toute magie: l'Amour.

Ils s'unissent et se mettent d'accord pour pardonner à la pauvre fée. Ni bonne, ni mauvaise. Seulement disgraciée. Puisque privée de cœur. Donc à plaindre. Malheureuse.

«Malheureuse comme la pierre», a-t-on coutume de dire. Et bien plus malheureuse encore que la pierre, notre fée. Car la pierre, elle, est amie du ruisseau, c'est certain.

Toutes leurs forces mises en commun, les hôtes de la forêt raniment la dame. Elle se réveille. Pitoyable. Elle s'éloigne en boitillant.

Personne ne la suit.

Magiquette émiette et jette au vent la baguette de bois mort.

Elle sait que, l'enchantement passé, elle va redevenir, elle est redevenue la petite poupée à l'œil vif, au sourire heureux.

Elle sait aussi que l'amitié des vivants, l'amitié de tous les habitants de la forêt l'a sauvée. Que l'amitié ici, et ailleurs, l'amitié lui est douce. Indispensable.

Pour vivre, pour bien se porter, pour bien vivre, il lui faut, il lui faudra l'amitié, toute l'amitié du monde. Celle de tous les vivants. Elle la gagnera, toute. Et la gardera. Toujours.

À force d'en donner, d'en prodiguer autour d'elle.

The Straw Doll

A RUMOR IS GOING AROUND IN THE FOREST THAT IN THE VILLAGE THERE is a little straw doll with bright eyes, porcelain teeth, and a happy smile. She sets off for school every morning with her sandwich in her hand and her bag on her back. Everyone wants to keep her company. That's because her little friends find her so pleasant.

Her old schoolteacher too is very fond of her. She is always saying: "Such a gifted and well-behaved pupil."

One afternoon during the holidays, the little doll goes for a walk in the countryside. The wind is singing in the branches and the leaves are dancing. For a moment, the little doll joins the green bushes in dance.

She stops in a glade and goes to sample the cool water of a spring. A line of mice file past in the grass. "Hello! Would you like to chat with us for a while?"

Since mice are always running about in the undergrowth, they must see a lot of things! Unfortunately they are always in a hurry. They barely have time to mutter a "Hi!" before moving off.

By chance, a blond fly is there looking quietly at, what?—a spider at work. She is extraordinarily skillful, this weaver! She is spinning an enormous parachute out of very fine thread.

"It must be fun to jump into that," says the fly. "I feel like trying it out." The little doll doesn't hear. She is listening to the voice of the brook that is hiding in a ditch. What a lovely stream! It forms a crown of bubbles on the pebbles set in the sand.

Maybe there are crayfish hiding in the stones. The little doll follows the current, to come up on the crayfish by surprise. But the stream goes on and on and the wood gets thicker and thicker. The little doll walks so much that she gets lost among the tree trunks. A real forest. But not like the other forests. This is an enchanted forest.

By the time it gets pitch black, the little doll is tired and has to sit down under a mushroom. What else can she do but go to sleep out in the open air?

The little doll is not fearful, but she is quite pleased to see a lady appear. A fairy, actually. Only you couldn't tell that right away. You couldn't tell either whether she is a good or wicked fairy. Perhaps neither one nor the other? Who knows? Right now, she stops and smiles at the little doll.

The squirrels well know that this lady is often frowning and looks wicked. When she passes, they prudently get out of sight. She is well known in the woods. Apparently they accuse her of not having a heart—or at least of having such a small heart that there is no room in it. Hardly any room except for one love—just the love she has for . . . herself. Oh yes, she has love for no one but her own self.

Alas, this evening everything in the neighborhood is already asleep. There is nobody who can whisper in the little doll's ear the fairy's names and nicknames. Some call her "Lady All-for-me." Others "Lady Heart-of-Ice." Since she likes to complain, she is sometimes called "Crocodile" or "Teary-Eyes."

Crocodile? Teary-Eyes? Oh no! As she is smiling now, this lady is beautiful! And charming! She easily leads away the sleepy little doll, who was already so tired.

The following morning when the little doll wakes up, it's hard for her to get over her shock. She doesn't recognize either the room or the bed, and certainly not the strange face of the woman leaning over her.

Where is she? What is she doing here? What happened to her? When? How? The more she questions herself, the more confused her memory becomes. Who is she, where does she come from? She has no idea. She has forgotten. She has forgotten everything.

The face in front of her is rather pleasant. It is beaming with pleasure. A new friend? That thought warms her heart. The little doll returns smile for smile. She thinks the fairy is nice and good.

Madame All-for-me whispers over and over to herself that fortune has brought her a fine gift. A pretty little lost doll, forsaken by everyone, it seems, with no mother, with no friends to protect her. A doll, moreover, looking innocent and warm-hearted.

One should make the most of the opportunity! Madame All-for-me will not fail. From now on, the little doll will be her servant, that's it. A kind of general factotum elf. And someone who will be obedient! A few words of the secret formula that she knows, a wave of a magic wand, and swish! The little elf will be ready to go. We'll start by calling her "Magiquette."

And Magiquette won't have a clue about what she will be expected to do. To begin with, she will have a beautiful life. And she will be allowed to do anything: to go for walks, to daydream in the woods, to go about free like a doe and chat with anyone she cares to.

And indeed, soon frogs in the swamps, crickets in the undergrowth, blackbirds in their nests, and bees around their hives all become her friends.

Whether they whistle, croak, coo, or cackle around her, Magiquette can understand everything that's said. And she can reply without any problem. They all want to tell her stories, teach her songs. She takes part in all the games. And so she comes to love her boon companions, and their neighbors, and their friends, and their cousins, and everything and everyone in the forest. Everybody. Including Madame All-for-me. As she goes out and comes home as she likes, Magiquette is the happiest little stuffed doll.

One day, while she is out walking she meets a snail. The lady in the shell passes right in front of her, turns back, goes forward, then turns back again. Odd behavior!

Intrigued, Magiquette stops. She doesn't dare question Mrs. Snail. It's the lady, who is a bit of a chatterbox, who speaks first: "You're not from here, are you?"

"No, Madame. Good day, Madame."

"Why do you call me 'Madame'? Call me 'Casodo' [House-on-Back] like everybody else. That would be nicer!"

"Yes, Madame Casodo!" They both burst out laughing at the same time. And all awkwardness between them disappears.

"Tell me, what's your name?"

"Now, I am Magiquette. I can't remember what my name was before."

"Her name from before. So she's changed it?" Casodo wonders, but she doesn't want to pry. She goes on in a casual tone:

"Why not Magiquette? That doesn't sound so bad! Since this is the first time we're seeing each other, I'm going to stop my work for a moment. To celebrate our meeting!"

"What kind of work are you doing there?"

"As you can see, I'm measuring the distance between the borders from one side of the road to the other."

"What borders?" Magiquette wonders. She can't see any. Casodo explains:

"My husband is the chief roadman. So when I go out for a walk, I mark the places for him where the borders should go. Afterwards he comes and puts them in. You will be sure to meet him if you pass by there. He won't be hard to recognize. He's a rather fat fellow, in spite of all his activity."

A snail that moves about a lot? That seems odd to the little doll. She almost chokes laughing. A big oaf who moves around like a bumblebee in a jar? Who has ever seen such a thing?

Casodo, more and more talkative, continues:

"My son is crushing stones over there where you've come from. Did you see him by the roadside?"

"No. I walked in the grass. Across the fields."

"So you didn't go through Insects' Village? A pity! Today is market day!

Market day? In Insects' Village? Magiquette's heart leaps for joy! That is something she absolutely has to see. To go for a walk in the village any morning must be really fun. But to go there on a market day? That would be truly exciting!

Of all live entertainment, Magiquette likes markets best. She likes to mingle with the gawkers. She likes to listen to the street vendors. She finds the displays beautiful: herbs, fruits, seeds, leaves, flowers, red, green, and yellow, arranged in piles on the tables. Looking like swaths of rainbows! Joy on sale by the slice!

And also the merchants are so funny sometimes! Stuck behind their stands, you can see them laughing, teasing one another, making fun of one another in a nice way. They interrupt their chatter to shout at passersby:

"My cherries, pure sugar, ladies! And my lettuce? Cost you next to nothing today, come and see!"

Even the clients are fun to watch! Especially the ladies. You see some bold ones who dive right into the piles, feeling the fruit in order to pick out the best ones. Others, more timid, hesitate. They fiddle with their purses, count their coins, feel their pockets. If Casodo would only show her how to get there, Magiquette would rush to the market!

Casodo is probably tired of working alone at the side of the road. She wants to take a break, of course, but Casodo wants even more to have someone listen to her. That's obvious.

Fortunately, the purring of an engine approaches. A lorry! At the wheel, a magnificent beetle. He stops by the little doll, who is still impatient to get away from Casodo. Greetings. Smiles! A ride to the market?

"With pleasure. I'm going in that direction! I'll put you down at the entrance of Insects' Village."

Beetle makes room for Magiquette. It's the first time that Magiquette has passed through this area. She has time to admire the scenery. The branches of the trees form an arch over the road. Magiquette is delighted. The driver is discreet and only occasionally speaks to her. Time passes. The sun climbs quickly to the middle of the sky.

When she reaches the village, Magiquette notices that many of the tradespeople have already started packing up. What a lot of cars! The village and the market are even larger than Magiquette had imagined.

The stalls are really like shops. The merchandise is often displayed in large cars whose hoods open to reveal what are in fact neatly organized shelves.

"The stallholders," Magiquette says to herself, "must certainly go around from place to place throughout the whole country. I have to find out somehow when and where they have their different market days."

In the meantime, she's all eyes. Lady Caterpillar tries out the salads. Lady Wasp haggles over fruit. Sturdy ants peddle sacks stuffed with grain. Lady Grasshopper, in a green blouse, waits in front of Mrs. Dragonfly, who is flanked by her twin daughters. She has unfurled an expensive piece of gauze before the client. Lady Dragonfly anxiously feels the material.

"Hurry up! Hurry up!" Mrs. Grasshopper's gesture clearly signifies. She clicks her large scissors impatiently.

Magiquette hurries to the bookstore. There too they are about to close. It's late. A gentleman in gray, a woodlouse?, sitting on a bench out of the way, is no doubt waiting for his wife to finish shopping.

Magiquette makes her way back home, skipping on one foot, preferably through the woods. When she reaches home, Mrs. All-for-me is not there. And Magiquette is disappointed. She has so many things to talk about. And so many joys to share!

The lady finally returns, and for Magiquette that's even more painful, because the fairy says she is not well. And it's the little doll's fault!

"I just left the doctor's. I thought you were lost in the woods and I was sick with fear! I was afraid that you'd met with some calamity so soon! The doctor had me take some pills. He gave me some injections and he's recommended rest for me. But no stress."

"You mustn't worry about me anymore," suggests Magiquette.

"If you were nice you wouldn't leave me too often. Or for too long. That would really relieve my mind."

Go for a walk only on certain days? So as to avoid causing her fairy friend any worry? Okay! Magiquette agrees that Tuesdays, Thursdays, and Saturdays from now on will be her holidays. The rest of the time she keeps busy in the house like a grown-up! She tidies, cleans, washes, mends, and doesn't get bored.

Last Thursday, Magiquette comes back home at sunset, as happy as a bee, and like a bee buzzing with good news. She had been playing with some pretty green tree frogs, three little cousins, Vivette, Vivaine, and Rennie, who invited her to go swimming with them. The water was deep, but the lake was very small! It was a nice little round lake, "where the sky looks at itself and smiles all the time," as Rennie would say.

Mrs. All-for-me listens, frowning. She doesn't reproach Magiquette for anything, but then talks about what she did. Just today, by chance, she wasn't feeling well. Thank God, it didn't last long, but there was no explanation for it. How to make sure it doesn't happen again? They don't know what caused it!

Magiquette on her own gives up going out one out of her three days—until things work out.

They change a lot of things, but to no avail. Bad things keep happening whenever the little doll is out. Soon there's only one step left to take: not to leave the house anymore.

Besides, the last time Magiquette went out, it wasn't very pleasant. Whom did she meet? Mansfrenil, all in black like an undertaker. Mansfrenil the sailor. You think he told a real sailor's story? Not at all. The big sad bird, Papa Gôh-Gôh, who is always shouting, "I'm thirsty, I'm thirsty," that's the adventure that Mansfrenil told Magiquette about.

You know, the springs, the rivers, the lakes, and even the ponds refuse to give their water to Gôh-Gôh. This bird can only drink when rain falls. Because it is a bird that has been cursed. Yes, cursed. Because it was wicked. Very wicked to Christ on the cross.

"I don't have anything like that to blame myself for," Magiquette says to herself. It would never occur to her to refuse to give anyone a glass of water. Particularly not to someone who is in pain, who has been hurt . . . When someone's lips have turned blue . . . you don't pass a sponge soaked in vinegar over their mouth! . . .

No. Magiquette hasn't found herself in such a situation. She would never do something like that . . . However, the poor little girl thinks about it. Suppose it were true that, without doing it on purpose, she had failed to be charitable toward the fairy? Suppose she had, out of thoughtlessness, omitted to do something nice or friendly, one thing, at the right time? Magiquette, afraid of causing something bad to happen, makes a resolution: she will not leave the house anymore. She will not go out to enjoy herself anymore!

And so it was that Lady All-for-me's tricks and Lady Crocodile's hypocrisy won out! From then on Magiquette would devote herself not just to obeying the fairy's orders, but to anticipating what she wanted. Just yesterday, did Madame feel like having a sorbet, a delicious cream dessert? Immediately, the wave of a wand, a magic formula! And Magiquette became a cordon-bleu cook!

Did she need a rubdown? A poultice? "Abracadabra!" Magiquette appeared dressed in a nurse's cap and gown!

And now, does madame want an elegant dress? A shawl for the cool nights, a song to take her mind off things? "Abracadabra" . . .

As soon as the first words are spoken, even before the wand moves, Magiquette is already stitching a dress, knitting a shawl, humming a melody.

After a while, Mrs. All-for-me doesn't know what else to ask for. Just for a change, she asks for sympathy.

Magiquette, happy to take care of her, to comfort her, becomes more and more zealous, more and more attentive.

One day, the fairy is bitten by a poisonous snake and finds herself in danger. For real. Her thoughts are not clear enough for her to remember the magic words. And Magiquette is not clever enough to find the needed remedy on her own.

Magiquette asks her friends in the forest for help. All of them go looking for herbs, roots, barks, to make up all kinds of ointments and teas. They turn the forest upside down. They consult the elders. They seek advice from the wise ones. To no avail.

Finally, Ara-the-Old speaks:

"We have tried all the known remedies, my friends. The only thing left to do is to try a magic elixir to attempt to save the sick one. I know a recipe . . . but we'd need to draw it from a living heart . . . It's very dangerous . . . The donor would be risking his life . . .

"You mean to say," cries Magiquette, "that all that's needed are living forces and you're hesitating?"

Before anyone could stop her, the crazy little one opens her chest. They quickly make the elixir and give it to Madame All-for-me.

She is cured. Fortunately, Magiquette recovers from her wound. She also gets better.

But now Madame Teary-Eyes develops a new bad habit. Pains in her hips, her legs, her head . . . She complains of a thousand new illnesses. Nothing ever gives her relief except a warm poultice made with straw.

She is always turning to Magiquette for help. The doll's arms and muscles are emptied of straw little by little.

Soon Lady Heart-of-Ice cannot wait for an excuse to get taken care of. She makes up something. For example, she just wants to "feel in good shape." Once, she goes as far as asking for straw "to get rid of the fleas on her favorite dog."

The lady makes so many demands that Magiquette's strength and vigor decline. The weaker the doll becomes, the more the Crocodile, weeping or smiling, asks for straw. More and more! For fun!

One day Madame All-for-me tries to water part of her garden. So that her tomatoes would grow very round and her lettuce would have good hearts!

Magiquette endures everything in secret. She doesn't complain to anyone. However, her friends are getting worried. Like a flower that has been severed from its stalk, the little doll is fading. She is slowly withering.

"We have to find a way to bring her strength back. And quickly!" declares Beetle.

He crisscrosses the whole country looking for a medicine. His large lorry goes over the roughest roads.

The inhabitants of the forest, when they become informed about the situation, all consult with one another. They hold their discussion under a tree that is more than one hundred years old—a giant catalpa. They each express their fears . . . give their opinion . . . offer their bit of wisdom.

The birds, big and small, in the course of their many voyages, have seen a lot and remembered a lot. Of course. But the trees? Didn't they take time to make observations, to reflect at length, hundreds and thousands of times? For years and years, in silence, and without moving, they have been gathering their thoughts and meditating!

The general discussion is animated. They are some chatterboxes, as you can well imagine, yes they are, among the birds! Finally, Grandfather Catalpa's voice is heard above all the others:

"None of us knows why our dear Magiquette has lost her health. None of us has been able to find a remedy to cure her. But if we put our strength together, we will be able to save her!

"When life is failing, it's because the heart is failing, yes or no?"

And they all shout together: "You're right!"

"So tell me, all of you, what's needed to restore vigor to the heart?"

And they all shout even louder: "Love! Love!"

"Since the strength to love is in the heart, the strength to live is also in the heart!"

"You're right! You're right!"

"So, listen, all of you. We great trees, we sink our roots into the black flesh of the earth. We raise up our heads . . . and thrust them into the blue of the sky. We are strong. But, in common with all of you, we have life. All of you! The frail baby birds . . . the flies with light wings, and the helpless larvae. All of us, from the most powerful to the weakest, we are all brothers. Rich with the same property: Life. And we're brothers to Magiquette, whom we love with the same heart.

"So, listen carefully, all of you—those of you whose blood burns red, as well as those of you whose sap rises clear . . . Listen and take an oath with me:

"As long as this day lasts, we sacrifice to Magiquette, our sister, that which is dearest to us, that which we love most in the world!"

With a single voice, all repeat the oath after Catalpa. All of them. Madame All-for-me like the others. "What do I stand to lose?" she thinks. "Since I don't love anyone or anything."

But she is mistaken. To be absolutely correct, she ought to specify: "I don't love anything or anyone besides myself."

That is how Madame All-for-me makes a promise, and utters an oath that commits her in a dangerous way. That is how her furious, terrible selfishness backfires on her. Since the only thing she loves is her own self, it's her own self that she has just committed. And has condemned. And places in mortal danger.

That day, as every hour slides on the dial, every hour brings roses back to Magiquette's cheeks. And every hour sees a wrinkle dug into Madame All-for-me's hard heart.

When the sun finally sets over the forest, everybody is left mute with surprise. Magiquette is restored to life and opens out like a new bud at sunrise.

Madame All-for-me, her eyes closed, keeps her hand open next to a wand of dead wood.

None of Magiquette's friends know the words of the magic formula that could perhaps awaken the unconscious lady . . . Or to bring its power back to the dried-up wand.

Even if they knew the secret words, would they care to use them? They have just discovered a much more important secret. There is in the world a power stronger than all the others, a magic more powerful than any magic: Love.

They come together in unity and agree to forgive the poor fairy. She's neither good, nor bad; only in disgrace, because she has no heart. Therefore she is unfortunate and to be pitied.

"Unfortunate like stone," was the usual saying. And even more unfortunate than stone is our fairy. For stone is certainly a friend of the streams.

Putting all their strength together, the occupants of the forest revive the lady. She wakes up. Pitifully, she goes off limping.

Nobody follows her. Magiquette breaks the deadwood wand into small pieces and scatters it to the wind.

She knows that, now that the spell is over, she is going to become again, she is already becoming again, the little doll with bright eyes and a happy smile.

She also knows that she was saved by the friendship of living creatures, by the friendship of all the inhabitants of the forest. That friendship, here and elsewhere, friendship is dear to her. Is indispensable.

To live, to be well, to live well, she needs, she will need, all the friendship in the world—the friendship of all living beings. And she will get all of it—and will keep it. Forever.

By giving it away, by spreading it around her.

Bibliography

CARBET, MARIE-MAGDELEINE

Chansonnelle. Fort-de-France: Jeunesse Cité du Livre, 1956.

Point d'orgue. Paris: La Productrice, 1958.

Ecoute Soleil-Dieu. Paris: Le Choix, 1961; Paris: Le Cerf-volant, 1974.

Viens voir ma ville. Paris: Le Productrice, 1963; Paris: Le Cerf-volant, 1974.

Suppliques et chansons. 1965; Paris: Le Cerf-volant, 1974.

Rose de ta grâce. 1970; Paris: Le Cerf-volant, 1974.

Au péril de ta joie. Montréal: Leméac, 1972.

Et merveille de vivre. Pontarlier: Faivre, 1973.

D'une rive à l'autre. Montréal: Leméac, 1975.

Comptines et chansons antillaises. Montréal: Leméac, 1975.

Mini-poèmes sur trois méridiens. Montréal: Leméac, 1977.

Au village en temps longtemps. Montréal: Leméac, 1977.

Le bon manger antillais. Montréal: Leméac, 1978.

La cuisine des isles. Verniers: Le Marabout, 1980.

Contes de Tantanta. Montréal: Leméac, 1980.

Au sommet, La sérénité. Montréal: Leméac, 1980.

CARBET, MARIE-MAGDELEINE, AND CLAUDE CARBET

Féfé et Doudou, Martiniquaises. Paris: CRES, 1936.

Chansons des isles. Paris: Orphée, 1937.

Piment rouge. Paris: Paul Mourousy, 1938.

Çà et là sur la Caraïbe. Paris: Ceux d'Outre Mer, 1938.

Braves gens de la Martinique. Paris: Cité du Livre, 1957.

HURLEY, E. ANTHONY

"Choosing Her Own Name, or Who Is Carbet?" *CLA Journal* 41, no. 4 (June 1998): 387–404.

"D'un masque à l'autre: Marie-Magdeleine Carbet." In *Elles écrivent des Antilles*, ed. Susanne Rinne and Joëlle Vitiello, 279–93. Paris: L'Harmattan, 1997.

"Intersections of Female Identity or Writing the Woman in Two Novels by Mayotte Capécia and Marie-Magdeleine Carbet." *French Review* 70, no. 4 (March 1997): 575–86.

"Marie-Magdeleine Carbet." In *Through a Black Veil: Readings in French Caribbean Poetry*, 45–120. Trenton, NJ: Africa World Press, 2000.

"Refusing Conformity: Marie-Magdeleine Carbet's Poetic Choices in *Point d'orgue*." *Degré Second: Studies in French Literature* 13 (December 1992): 65–72.

Afterword

On Translating Carbet

Marie Magdeleine Carbet's project in writing short stories was to inject Martinican folk culture into the larger corpus of French literary tradition and thus validate the Martinique identity and cultural expression. Martinican folk culture, however, features as one of its essential elements the language of the Martinican folk—i.e., Creole. Translating Carbet's short stories, therefore, means translating Martinican folk culture and transposing it into a cultural equivalent within an Anglophone, including AngloAmerican, context. Standard English, even standard American English, would not be equivalent. The challenge for the translator, therefore, is to find an equivalent linguistic register that bearsa similar relationship to standard English and American English that Carbet's language bears to standard French. Of relevance to this discussion is the TransAtlantic (sAlt) translation theory, pioneered by Dr. Janis Mayes of Syracuse University, which relies on the translator's capacity to be familiar with and to negotiate the specific cultural and linguistic (e.g., Kamau Brathwaite's "nation language") spaces that are unique to the African diaspora.

Thanks to the French Academy, French is fairly rigidly standardized, unlike English, including American English. Caribbean English vernaculars can, however, fairly easily be distinguished from the various standardized Englishes, in relation to idiomatic expression, syntactic structures, and lexicon. In order to "translate" Carbet's creolized French with a degree of accuracy and fidelity to the larger geocultural context, therefore, it is necessary to be familiar with the ways in which Carbet's usage of French deviates from standard French and also with expressions in the Anglophone Caribbean vernacular that would occupy a similar position vis-à-vis standard English.

The following illustrations are pertinent. One of the stories in this volume was originally published in a collection of short stories titled *Contes de Tantana*, and "Tantana" appears as a character in several of Carbet's narratives. The appellation "Tantana" (meaning familiarly Aunt Anna) is clear in Creole and perhaps even in French. It is, however, less so in English, Black American English, or in Anglophone Caribbean (Jamaica, Barbados), though it is recognizable in Caribbean territories with some French colonial background (St. Lucia, Dominica, etc.). Over the past forty years or so, the Grenadian storyteller Paul Keens-Douglas spread stories of "Tantie Merle" throughout the Caribbean and Caribbean populations in Canada and England. The popularity of these stories has extended the understanding and acceptance of "Tantie." So that "Tantie Anna" would translate with a fair degree of cultural accuracy Carbet's use of "Tantana."

Carbet titled another of her short stories, "Le «Quimbois»." We know that this term indicates the cultural practice common to African-heritage populations throughout the Americas, variously associated with the application of natural or supernatural means to change one's circumstances. The question, however, is how to translate the term in "English." Whether one uses "witchcraft," "sorcery," "working roots," "vaudou," or "obeah," the decision reflects the privileging of a cultural perspective—Anglo-Caribbean and Franco-Caribbean, African American, etc. My decision to use "obeah" inevitably and deliberately privileges an Anglo-Caribbean perspective.

Other examples would include Carbet's use of Creole expressions ("Qui nove"), Creole songs (*Moin planté pensées/C'est soucis moin récolté*), and Creole proverbs ("Zaffai cabrite pas zaffai mouton"). They all present the same challenge: which linguistic equivalent, representing a cultural privileging, to use—Anglo-Caribbean Creole or Standard or African American English.

These decisions invite contemplation of what I consider to be cultural and academic questions or challenges that generally confront the translator. First, the question of readership. Who is the intended audience, readership of the translation? It is easy to assert that this readership will be English-speaking. But for French Caribbean texts, there is a considerable cultural and linguistic gulf between Anglo-American, Anglo-African, African American, and Anglo-Caribbean readers. An "English Caribbean" translation can in many respects be as "foreign" to the Anglo-American reader as the original French version. The challenge therefore is to find a way of bridging that gap. One device, always awkward, is the use of footnotes or a glossary to explain either the terms used in the source text or the translation or both. Another possibility is to leave the ambiguity or unfamiliarity in the translated version, so that the reader could experience the same "discomfort" that the French reader would have experienced when first confronted with the source text. Carbet herself has employed some of these devices in the "original" or source text, indicating her awareness of the need for some "translation" even at that primary stage.

Within the context of the structure of academic institutions, there is, furthermore, the larger question of the inclusion of some works translated into English in offerings by so-called English departments. In my institution, for instance, there is some resistance to permitting students to take cross-listed courses in texts translated from the French or Spanish Caribbean as part of their English major. In other words, such English translations are not accepted as "English," while translations of canonical Russian novels are accepted.

Finally, as a kind of inconclusive conclusion, we may recall that Fanon, in *Peau noire, masques blancs*, alludes to the importance of language in the colonial context, as a vector of cultural values. We may also recall that a dominant feature of the European (Italian as well as Greco-Roman) Renaissance of the fifteenth century, which marked the flourishing of creative activity by which European civilization would henceforth be privileged to assess its own global significance, was massive translation, or what has been referred to a "traslatio studii"—that is, the wholesale, literal taking across borders: the kidnapping, the hijacking of cultural knowledge, cultural artifacts, across geographical and linguistic borders (from North Africa, including Egypt, and what we now call the Middle East); and then appropriating them to create what was called a "Renaissance" or rebirth. Maybe it is only coincidental that the hijacking of Africans by the Portuguese started around the same time. Africans were indeed translated, and it would not be too far-fetched to argue that the appropriation of the cultural expertise of Africans contributed enormously to the new civilization of the New American World.

The question all translators face, whether we realize it or not, is that to some extent, whatever our motives may be, we may be participating in a similar exercise.